The Perfect
Escape
(Sinful Pleasures #2)

A.L. Long

Editor: H. Elaine Roughton
Cover Design: Elena Krishtop
Formatting: Allongbooks
Publisher: Allongbooks

Acknowledgment

To my wonderful husband, who is with me heart, body and soul through each word I write. If it weren't for him my dream of writing would have never been fulfilled. I love you, sweetheart. And to my family, whom I also love dearly. Through their love and support, I can continue my passion for writing.

To the many readers, who took a chance on me and purchased my books. I hope that I can continue to fill your hearts with the passion I have grown to love.

Most of all I want to thank my incredible PA, Barbara Danks. I don't know where I would be without her and to my wonderful Street Team (Athena Kelly, Lori Hammons, Kristen Ann Tanner, Marsha Black, Sallie Ann, Andrea Miles Rhoads). You ladies have been a godsend.

Synopsis

Some would say that revenge is nothing more than returning the favor, but for me it is much more than that.

Reyna McCall may have been my only leverage against the man who took everything from me, but now she is much more than that.

 The game has changed and so have the players, but not even that will stop me from getting her back.

My rules, my way. There is only room for one winner.

From Award-Winning author A.L. Long comes an explosive dark romance surrounded by lies and deceit. The Perfect Escape is the second installment to the Sinful Pleasures Series. It is recommended you read The Perfect Wife (Sinful Pleasures #1)

Warning

This book contains adult language and scenes that are sexual or physical abusive and are not suitable for young readers. It may cause trigger reactions and is only intended for adults, as defined by law in the country in which you live.

Prologue

Reyna

The definition of love was a funny thing. My adoptive mom always told me that one day I would meet the perfect man, get married, and give her lots of grandchildren. She got one thing right; I was married, but not to a man I loved, let alone wanted to be in the same room with. The only man that meant anything to me was over nine hundred miles away, out of reach.

Three weeks had passed since Rui took me against my will. I finally understood where my place was. *Seen, but not heard.* It was the only way I would survive under Rui Salko's control. At least he wasn't around as much as when I first entered his home. He hadn't touched me, other than a kiss here and there, which made my stomach turn. I was positive that my mouth was the cleanest one in the house since I couldn't stand the taste of him. I was glad when he left, especially when his work took him away for a few days at a time. With him away, it meant he wouldn't be touching me or disciplining me. If he wasn't kissing me, he was punishing me for not following his instructions. He was a monster, and not even the makeup could hide the marks he left to remind me of my place.

The front door slammed with a loud crash, signaling his arrival, but more than that, his mood. My heart jumped, knowing it wouldn't be such a great day for me. I could always tell how well Rui's trips went from the way he closed the door. I never knew from one day to the next if he would return or what his mood would be, but I always prepared myself for the worst.

Shivers ran down my body as I heard the angry tone in his voice. "Reyna, I'll be taking my dinner in the study."

Holding my breath, I pulled the roast out of the oven. "Okay, Rui. I'll have it done in fifteen minutes." When Rui gave the staff time off, learning how to cook was one of the many things he demanded of me. With the cooking staff's help, before Rui put them on leave, I had quickly learned how to prepare his meals. Without knowing if he would show up, I always made enough for two. Most of the time, the leftovers were thrown away. Rui didn't tolerate having to eat reheated food. I learned that early on.

It wasn't unusual for Rui to take his dinner in his study, and I preferred it when he did. It allowed me to avoid his sarcastic remarks about how thankful I should be that I was with him instead of Davian.

Almost always, Rui would bring his work home. I

wasn't sure exactly what the mafia required of him, but I didn't care. He would focus on it instead of me, and I would be safe from his wrath.

Dishing Rui's plate just the way he liked, with meat at two o'clock, bread at ten, and vegetables at six, I wiped off the excess juice that fell onto the plate before placing it on the serving tray. Adding two ice cubes to his Scotch, I set the glass above the silverware and made sure the glass lined up with the knife and was free of any water spots.

I shook my hands to ease the nervousness and took hold of the tray. I steadied the tray as I walked to Rui's study. The door was slightly open, and the last thing I wanted was to disturb him while he was working. Taking a chance, I pushed the door open with my shoulder. I looked over to the window, where I found him sitting at his large mahogany desk. It was always dark in his study, except for the only light he allowed which was from the lamp on his desk. Of all the rooms in the house, his study was the single room where he demanded the curtains be closed. Only once I had opened them to bring in the sunlight. In return, he slapped my cheek. The bruise Rui left was a reminder. Even today, it was still visible, even with makeup.

I thought he hadn't heard me come in until he lifted his head, and his stone-cold eyes met mine. "You're late with my dinner, Reyna. It had better be good."

I continued to walk toward the coffee table that sat

between four wing-back chairs, two on each side. I couldn't stop my hands from shaking, concerned that if I didn't control them, I would end up dropping the tray. My eyes focused on the Scotch sloshing back and forth against the glass as I carefully lowered the tray onto the table. As I stepped away from the table, ready to make my escape, I crashed into Rui's hard body. His eyes weren't on me, but on the table. "It seems you have forgotten how to follow instructions."

Grabbing me by the back of my neck, he pushed my head toward the table and made me look at the tray. Everything on the plate had shifted. An average person wouldn't have noticed, but Rui did. Before I could explain, his free hand came across my face, which made me lose my balance. Unable to break the fall, I fell sideways onto the coffee table. The edge of the table dug into my side, and all I could do was watch the tray tumble to the floor, shattering the glass of Scotch and the plate into a million pieces as it hit the hard floor. Pushing away from the table, I held back the pain the fall had caused and tried to stand. Instead of showing concern, Rui was more worried about the mess I caused. "Clean up this mess. I'm going out."

Once he left, I fell to my knees and began picking up the larger pieces of glass before tackling the smaller ones. As hard as I tried, the strain of the last three weeks of being under this man's control broke loose, and the tears fell. I didn't want to shed one more tear because of this monster. It didn't matter what I did. Nothing would be good enough for

Rui Salko.

I could handle the constant abuse. It was his words that took me further and further away from the person I was. I was lucky to escape with only a bloody lip or a bruised cheek. If I weren't so afraid of him, I would fight back. I had to find a way to escape. In reality, Davian wouldn't be coming to get me. I had to do this on my own if I wanted to live.

A loud noise startled me, and I rolled over to my side to find that the alarm clock read 5:00 a.m. I had cleaned the mess I made in the study over eight hours ago, and I wasn't sure if Rui had come home yet. As I pushed to my feet to investigate what caused the noise, I noticed a large figure in the doorway to my bedroom. It was Rui. He didn't say a word as he walked over to the bed. Women's perfume laced with alcohol lingered in the air as he stood beside the bed. I avoided eye contact and headed to the bathroom to get a drink of water.

When I returned, I should have been angry, but I wasn't. Rui's body stretched across the bed. He was out. I didn't dare wake him. I should have been thankful that he had passed out, and another woman got his attention instead of me, but all it did was make me sick. She was surely another victim of his wrath.

I left the room and carefully shut the door. Instead of catching more sleep, I decided to get a jump on finding a way to leave this place, once and for all. Rui would be out for hours, and since it was Saturday, the alarm in my room wouldn't be going off to wake him since I hadn't set it. I had only a short window of opportunity to search the house for a phone. I could have searched his body for his cell, but I feared that I would wake him and he would finally take what he hadn't in three weeks. As I headed down the stairs, I decided to check his office first.

Closing the door behind me, I worked my way to his desk in the darkness by taking slow, careful steps with my hands in front of me. When Rui's desk hit my legs, I had reached it. Turning on the desk lamp, I waited for my eyes to adjust to the light before rounding the desk. I pulled out every drawer hoping to find something, anything that would help with my escape. Staring down at the only drawer I hadn't tried, I gripped the handle, but it wouldn't budge. Rui locked it. None of the other drawers held a key, so it was either on Rui's person or hidden somewhere else. Scanning the top of his desk for anything that I could pry the drawer open with, I spotted a letter opener beneath a stack of papers. Working the letter opener between the drawer and the desk, I was finally able to pry it open.

As I pulled the drawer free, my breath hitched as a gun stared back at me, lying on top of some other papers.

Lifting it with my thumb and my index finger, I put it on top of the desk. I didn't hate guns, but I hated what they could do. I slide my hand under the papers, and something hard hit my fingers. It was a phone. As I pulled it out, I saw it was a flip phone. My eyes widened with hope until I flipped it open. I tried to bring it to life, but it was dead. I leaned against the back of the chair, all the air leaving my body in disappointment. I had to keep searching. There had to be a cord to charge it somewhere. Leaning forward, I pulled the papers from the drawer where I found the phone. I reached towards the back, and my fingers pulled out the cord. My heart fluttered with excitement.

When I was about to leave Rui's office, I heard my name. "Reyna, where the fuck are you?"

Turning off the light, I crawled underneath his desk and remained still. If he found me in his study, he would undoubtedly kill me. Somehow, I needed to get to my room, but how? It sounded like he was still upstairs, and I couldn't stay under his desk forever. Sooner or later, he would find me. I had to move. Sliding out from under his desk. I slowly crawled on my hands and knees to the door. When I didn't hear his voice again, I carefully turned the knob and pulled the door open. The phone and cord were still in my hand as I made my way to the kitchen. It would be the one room he wouldn't question me being in. Once there, like a dutiful wife, I would answer his question about my whereabouts.

The lights were off when I reached the kitchen.

Before switching on the lights, I searched for a place to hide the phone and cord. I couldn't risk Rui finding them on me when he came down the steps after hearing where I was. The time of the morning provided very little light, but I remembered a small accent table with a drawer beneath a painting near the staircase. It was a risk, but it would be the safest place to hide it until I could get to it later.

Once I placed the phone and cord safely in the drawer, I headed back to the kitchen. Even if he came down the stairs, I would be safe with my explanation. Reaching around the corner, I switched on the light.

I gasped with surprise as I heard Rui's words. "Why the fuck didn't you answer me?" His eyes were on mine, and a rage of anger I had never seen sent a chill down my spine.

My body was shaking with fear, and I was unable to speak. Rui's eyes grew darker as he stood from a kitchen chair and walked toward me. My mind was telling me to run, but my body wouldn't move. Without warning, he pressed my body against the wall, and his hand went to my throat. I couldn't breathe, but somehow answered his question. "I was upstairs. I didn't want to wake you, so I used the guest bathroom."

"You're lying. Just like your mother."

Before I could explain further, he released the grip

on my throat and replaced it with the back of his hand against my cheek. I wobbled from the blow, but remained upright. The taste of metal tinged my mouth, and I was sure he had split my lip. *No tears... Reyna, No tears.*

When he placed his hand on my cheek, my head jerked, a response to getting hit again. Smiling, he leaned in, his whiskey breath close to my ear. "You are a beautiful woman, my sweet Reyna. Don't give me a reason to kill you. I would hate for you to end up like your mother." The feel of him pressing his lips to mine made the bile in my throat rise. "I'm going to shower. When I return, I trust you will have breakfast ready for me. I'll take it in the garden."

When he left the kitchen, my body fell to the floor. I hated him. Even though he didn't come out and admit it, he killed my mom. I was sure of it. *Stay strong, Reyna. Your days with him are almost over.*

~1~

Five years ago

Davian

"Gwen, sweetheart. If you don't hurry, we're going to be late. My father went to a lot of trouble to plan the reception dinner." The last thing I wanted was to piss off my father by being late.

"I know, Davian. It's just that I want to look my best."

Little did she know, she was already beautiful. As I stepped behind her, I reminded her of just that. "You're gorgeous, baby. My father already loves you, and so do the guys."

It wasn't a lie. Gwen's beauty surpassed the word gorgeous. From the day I met her at Cross Enterprises, I had to have her. She was the daughter of Crosby and Delilah McCall, both very close friends of my father's. My father hired Gwen to head the legal department at Cross Enterprises after she graduated from the University of

Chicago with a JD in business law. It wasn't her intelligence that attracted me. It was her beautiful green eyes. Like rare uncut emeralds, they glistened every time she smiled or when a ray of light hit them just right.

Fidgeting with her long blonde hair, she finally gave up and pulled it into a long ponytail, securing it with a hair tie at her neck. She wrapped a few strands around the tie and secured it with a bobby pin. It was simple but elegant and matched the black sheath dress she finally chose to wear after three dress changes. Personally, I thought all three were gorgeous on her.

We headed out the door, tipping very close to being late. If we hurried, we could make it in time to get our menu order in. My father harped on punctuality. But the way Gwen looked, even he would let it slide. My father always had a soft spot for beautiful women.

Twenty minutes later, with less than five minutes to spare, we were at the restaurant and escorted to the back room, which my father reserved for the Cross party of twelve. Before we made it past the doorway, ten sets of eyes were on us. Crosby and Delilah McCall sat at the far end of the long table, closest to the wall, while the rest of the Cross men, Marcus, Calvin, Patton, Sean, and Axe, occupied five of the remaining seats. Next to Axe sat Gwen's maid of honor, Eve, and next to her was Mika. Only three seats remained—one at each end of the table, which my father and I took, and the seat next to Patton, which Gwen took.

Gwen's other girlfriends, Kimberly, Becca, and Elena, who would have completed the wedding party, decided planning Gwen's bachelorette party was more important. Otherwise, it would have ended up as Cross party of fifteen. On this of all nights, the girls insisted on surprising Gwen with her bachelorette party. It didn't matter what I thought. Bound and determined, nothing would have stopped them.

Above everything, I wanted them to have fun, but I also wanted to make sure they stayed safe. I told Eve to let me know where they would be and let me know if they left and went somewhere else. Taking the extra precaution, Axe and Calvin would be there, remaining out of sight, in case the girls ran into any problems. I hated to think about what would happen if Gwen found out they had two babysitters.

The dinner conversation was light, focusing on where the groomsmen would stay while Gwen and her bridesmaids got ready. The wedding wasn't a traditional church wedding. Gwen and I decided the Cross Estate would be the perfect place for a wedding. When Gwen told Mika of our plans, Mika jumped for joy. Not only because the wedding was taking place at the estate, but also because Gwen had chosen her to be one of her bridesmaids. The way Mika's eyes lit up when Gwen told her what we had planned warmed my heart. Mika had enough excitement for the both of us. The thought of spending the rest of my life with Gwen was a dream come true. I loved her more than life itself, and I would spend every day showing her just how much.

While I was holding those thoughts close to my heart, I realized the pre-rehearsal dinner had ended. Soon, Gwen and Eve would be with the rest of the girls celebrating Gwen's last night out as a single woman. Tomorrow night, Patton, Calvin, Marcus, Sean, Axe, and I would have our night to celebrate. Even though they all worked for Cross Enterprises, they were all friends. They were men that I respected, risking their lives, protecting our country. I would have been right there with them if it hadn't been for a fluke accident, which left me legally blind in one eye. I could have fought the military on it, but I didn't want to sit behind a desk all day when all I wanted was to fight for my country on the front line.

After kissing Gwen goodbye and reminding her to be careful, I watched them drive away before getting in my car. I wasn't ready to drive back to the Cross Estate, so instead, I drove to the pier. It was the best place to go to clear my head. In a couple of weeks, Gwen would be my wife, and we could finally begin our lives together. Two years of being engaged were two fucking years too long. I respected Gwen's decision to wait until she finished undergraduate school and passed the bar, but damn if I didn't want us married the very minute I set eyes on her.

There was something about the pier that always gave me the peace of mind I needed. Sure, my life was going to change, but damn if I wasn't ready. I only wished that my mom could be there to share it with me. I was dreaming. She would never get better, at least not enough to remember me.

After walking for what seemed like hours, I headed back to Cross Estate. The time was approaching 1:00 a.m., and Gwen would be home keeping our bed warm, waiting for me to take her. Just the thought tented my trousers.

As I pulled up to the estate, it was obvious something was off. The gate to the estate was open. I gave specific instructions to make sure the gate was closed at all times. Putting my car into park, I stepped out and walked over to the security booth where Theo patrolled the entrance. When I opened the door, the chair he always occupied was empty. "Damn. What the hell?" I said with only the night air to hear me.

Going back to my car, I was about to open the door when I saw a figure walking toward me. As I kept my eyes on the private road leading to the estate, the outline of a large frame neared. As he got closer, I could see it was Theo coming toward me. He kept his head lowered, with his hands resting in his pockets. When he looked up, there was nothing more unnerving than the look on his face.

Standing face to face with me, Theo was silent. "What is going on, Theo?"

It wasn't often that he was at a loss for words, but when his jaw turned tight and strained, it was evident that something was wrong. "It's Ms. Gwen, Mr. Cross."

Theo didn't need to say another word. I heard it in

his voice. Turning away from Theo, I headed to my car and got in. It was a short drive to the house, but every passing second was one second too long.

Cars parked front to back overtook the circular drive, but my sights were only on one. The police car I parked behind was unmarked, and there was only one reason it was here. Throwing my car into park, I headed up the steps two at a time. I reached for the handle to the door, but my shaky hand prevented me from turning the handle. Whatever awaited me beyond the door, my gut told me it would tear me in two.

When I stepped into the living room, it looked like nothing more than a social gathering. I knew better. The somberness was thick. This was a vigil, and Gwen was the only person not in attendance. I couldn't accept what I was witnessing. Looking at my father, I asked, "Where is Gwen?"

When my father walked over to where I was standing, it was clear. I stared back at him when he placed his hand on my shoulder. "I think it's best if you take a seat."

"I don't want to take a seat. I want to know where Gwen is." Every emotion filtered through my body, and my father took the brunt of it. "Where the fuck is Gwen?"

As I looked around the room for answers, I saw the

women's eyes were filled with tears while the men's faces stayed dry, contorted with grief. Before my father could answer, a man I didn't recognize stepped behind my father. "I'll take it from here, Lorenzo."

Looking at the man, I waited for answers. "My name is Detective Olson," he announced, clearing his throat before he continued. "I'm sorry to inform you, Mr. Cross, but we found Gwen McCall's body in the alley behind Harper's Corner Bar. We believe someone forced her outside and later killed her."

The detective walked over to where I was standing and placed his hand on my shoulder. "I know this is a lot to digest, but we need you to identify her. Mr. and Mrs. McCall are unavailable, and we need confirmation that it is her."

I couldn't comprehend what the detective said. It had to be nothing more than a bad dream. Nothing else made sense. Gwen wasn't dead, and the woman he wanted me to identify was someone else's daughter.

Fiancée.

Entire world.

Looking over to Axe and Calvin, I ignored the detective's request. "How could this happen? You were supposed to keep an eye on the girls and make sure they were safe."

Axe stepped out from behind the couch, his eyes never leaving mine. "You're right, and we were. There was nothing to make us suspect that Gwen was in any danger. We only lost sight of her for a moment when she went to the ladies' room. You wanted us to stay out of sight. It wasn't an option to follow her to the bathroom. One of us should have followed her. She would still be alive."

The sound of a cell phone filled the room, interrupting our conversation. The detective pulled his phone from his pocket and answered the call. After a few words, he placed it back inside his pocket. "I'm afraid my presence is required at the station. Mr. Cross, as soon as you can get down to Mercy General to identify Ms. McCall's body, the better."

As soon as Detective Olson left, I knew I needed more answers than the ones I got. The girls didn't need to hear what I had to say. "Men, in the library, now."

When the last man entered and secured the door behind him, my questions began. "Tell me everything you know and leave nothing out."

I heard everyone had a coping mechanism built inside their brain to deal with a tragic event. Mine was to find the motherfucker who killed my fiancée. Every detail, no matter how big or small, would be investigated. I didn't get where I was today by being sloppy. Every course of action needed to be taken to find out who did this.

I was waiting patiently for someone to speak up when Axe stepped forward. "When Gwen didn't come back to the table where the rest of the girls were, I got nervous. I headed back to where the restrooms were and asked a woman waiting in line for the bathroom to find out if anyone inside named Gwen was still in there. When the woman came out with no response to Gwen's name, I went to the back door to the bar."

Axe's voice broke, his emotions getting the best of him. "Sorry, Davian. If I would have checked on her sooner or waited outside the restroom for her, she would still be alive."

I stepped up to Axe and placed my hand on his shoulder. "I'm not blaming you, Axe. I just want to find the son-of-a-bitch who took her away from me and give him the same courtesy he gave Gwen."

With a nod of his head, Axe gathered his composure and continued where he left off. "When I opened the door, I looked around. I didn't spot her right away, so I walked down the alley. That's when I found her. Whoever killed her propped her body up against the brick wall beside a dumpster. There was blood everywhere. Her face took most of the abuse. I knew it wasn't a mugging since she still had her engagement ring. So, before I called the police, I gathered as much evidence as I could. Anything that could lead us to who did this to her."

"Where is this evidence now?" I asked.

"In the trunk of my car. And..." Axe's hesitation drew me to one conclusion.

When Axe handed me his phone, my hand shook as I scrolled through the pictures he took. All I saw was the woman I loved, beaten, most likely terrified beyond belief. Her death was on me. I wasn't there to protect her. Just like Axe described, someone had propped her body up against the brick wall—put on display. I'd seen this before. Only one name came to mind: Salko. The bastard killed Gwen, and he just signed his own death sentence. I only hoped that Axe got the evidence we needed to bury his ass.

~2~

Present Day

Davian

My patience was depleting by the minute. Margaret Curtis skated around every question I asked her, pushing me closer to the edge. Maybe she didn't have a clue who Rui Salko was, but my gut told me she wasn't as innocent as she appeared.

"I find it hard to believe, Ms. Curtis, that you just happened to be assigned to Reyna Braxton's case and also her adoption."

"I'm telling you the truth. I was assigned as Reyna's caseworker by the state."

Years of smoking hadn't done Margaret Curtis justice. She looked much older than fifty-nine. From the looks of it, she would have been an attractive woman, but the addictive habit won out. Lighting one cigarette after the other, her nervous behavior proved she had something to hide.

"Where is your brother?" My hand came down on

the table, causing her to jump. I needed answers. This cat-and-mouse game was over.

"He's in Atlanta. That's all I know. I swear."

"Give me your cell phone." One way or another, I would find Giles Curtis. If Margaret Curtis kept in touch with her brother, his number would be in her recent contacts.

Her hand shook as she handed me her phone. When I swiped the screen, it showed a locked screen requiring a password. "What's the damn password?"

Margret only hesitated for a moment, until Patton moved closer to where she sat, intimidating her to give it up. "1961."

Unbelievable. Margaret Curtis used the year she was born as her password. Not very smart on her part. Punching in the numbers, I brought her phone to life. Just as I suspected, no more than 30 minutes ago, she contacted her brother. I handed her phone back to her. It didn't take long to figure out who Brax was. "Call your brother."

After Margaret completed the call under my instructions, we had a meeting place. I had to hand it to her; she did exactly as I asked, with no visible sign of nervousness. With her phone in hand, we left her grungy doublewide trailer. Patton saw no evidence of a landline in the trailer, so there was no risk that she would call her brother back to warn him it was a set-up. Even if she found another way to contact him, which I was sure she would, it would have been a stupid move on her part. Hopefully, threatening her job was incentive enough to make her think twice. Margaret Curtis denied giving her brother information on Reyna's adoption, but my gut said she did.

As we got into the car, Patton looked over to me. "I don't know about you, boss, but I need a shower."

"I agree. Meet me back at the Regency at noon." Disgusted as well, I got what he meant. In the span of our brief chat with Ms. Curtis, she smoked half a dozen cigarettes. At fifty-nine, her addiction made her look twenty years older.

Heading over to a park bench near the Androgyne Planet sculpture, I waited for Giles Curtis to show up. Patton was seated across the fountain, keeping an eye out. We both had no clue what Curtis looked like other than a photo Patton pulled from the Internet from sixteen years ago. He was one of those men who was hard to miss. Just like the men in *The Society,* he had a military background. I had never met the man, but my father told me that Giles Curtis was Salko's right-hand man and did all of his dirty work.

Pushing back my shirt cuff, I looked down at my watch to see that it was 1:45 p.m., which meant that Giles Curtis was fifteen minutes late. My gut told me he wouldn't be showing up. There was no reason for him to suspect that he was meeting someone other than his sister unless Margaret Curtis tipped him off. Pulling her phone from my pocket, I swiped the screen and entered her four-digit password. I couldn't call him, but it didn't mean that I couldn't send him a text. Typing a message as though it was his sister showing concern, I waited for him to respond.

Margaret's cell vibrated instantly with an incoming call. I could have just let it go to voice mail, but if I didn't answer it, he just might show up at Margaret's house and find out it wasn't her who sent him the text.

Swiping the screen to answer the call, I remained silent as he spoke. "I know it's you, Cross, and you just fucked up. The minute my sister called me, I knew something was wrong. She knows not to call or text me."

How could I have missed that all the calls were incoming and not outgoing?

"Curtis, I only want to talk. Nothing more. Your boss has something of mine, and I want it back."

There was silence, and I had a feeling he was considering meeting me. Nothing would make me happier than to find out what his connection was to Reyna and if he knew where Salko might have taken her.

"I'll meet you, but on my terms." Curtis just made a wise choice. Probably the best choice in his pathetic life.

"Where?"

After getting the directions to the location where Curtis wanted to meet, I walked over to Patton, who was still waiting on the other side of the fountain. When I approached him, it didn't take long for him to realize that something was up. "Let me guess. Giles Curtis is a no show."

"Not exactly. He wants to meet in Gainesville, where Reyna used to live." I found it odd that he would choose Reyna's childhood home as the place he wanted to meet.

"Seems kind of strange that he would want to meet there, don't you think?" Patton scratched his bald head before pacing in a complete circle.

"I know what you're thinking, Patton, but we both know we don't have a choice. If it could help us find Reyna, we have to go."

After leaving the park, we had a few hours before we had to leave for Gainesville. It was only an hour's drive, and before we left, I thought it best to see if we could track where Curtis was just before he called.

As we pulled inside the warehouse, I could see Axe and Calvin sitting in the computer room through the entrance door. Upon my instructions, Marcus was monitoring Margaret's trailer in the event she left, while Sean remained Kenzi's shadow. I was pretty sure she wasn't in danger since Salko got his revenge when he took Reyna. On the other hand, he was still crazy and unstable, and I didn't want to take the chance that I was wrong.

For now, my top priority was to find out where Curtis was. Axe and Calvin were both computer geniuses, but Patton was the master hacker. There wasn't anything that he couldn't hack. If the information was out there, Patton knew how to get it. After I gave him Margaret's phone on the way over, he wasted no time finding out where her asshole brother was. If he was still in Atlanta, it would save us a trip to Gainesville.

Patton and I each pulled up a chair in front of a vacant computer. I focused my sights on his magic fingers as he began typing away at the keyboard. Bringing Margaret's phone to life, Patton entered the password and pulled up her brother's contact information. He resumed typing, and a series of numbers appeared on the screen. I had no clue what they meant, but small dots appeared when Patton opened another app with a map. It was a map of Atlanta. "What the hell?" Patton cursed as he continued typing on the keyboard.

"Tell me what you see, Patton." Whatever the

numbers on the screen meant, he knew the answer.

"I don't get it. It's like Curtis is in a hundred places all at once. It's impossible. His cell is bouncing off of all the towers." Pushing away from the desk, he tilted his head back, rubbing his hands over his face.

"What could cause this?" I asked as the dots multiplied.

"He has to be using a jammer. It is the only explanation." Patton pulled himself back to the table and began typing on the keyboard.

The screen went completely black before it lit up again. The numbers were no longer multiplying by the hundreds. Only one number popped up—Margaret's. "Shit," Patton quickly unplugged the computer and pushed away from the desk. "Shut down all the computers. Now!"

Axe and Calvin were up off their seats, scrabbling to turn off all the computers while Patton struggled to pull the tracker from Margaret's phone. When every computer screen had gone black, Patton turned to face me. "I think we stopped it in time."

"Stopped what?" I looked at him, completely confused by what happened in a matter of minutes.

"Curtis. He had to have known we would try to

locate his position. He used the information I was entering to locate our position by using Margaret's phone. He knew she didn't have it. And we did."

"Shit." I was the one raking my hand through my hair. Giles Curtis was smarter than I gave him credit for. I should have known better. He worked for Salko. It looked as though we would be heading to Gainesville after all. "Pack the Explorer. I'm not about to be blindsided again."

~3~

Reyna

After Rui had finished his breakfast, he spent most of his time in his study. For that, I was thankful. It was nearly 1:00 p.m., and I still hadn't been able to retrieve the cell I had hidden inside the drawer of the accent table near the stairs. It was my only hope of getting out of here, and I just couldn't chance getting caught.

As I prepared a light lunch, I tried to think positive thoughts. Davian would never leave me with this man. Once he found out where I was, he would come for me. And since there was no way for him to get in touch with me, I had to reach out to him. Hopefully, Rui would leave on one of his business trips, and I could get to the phone and charge it long enough to call Kenzi. Her number was the only one that I knew by heart. Growing up, I never memorized my home number. I should have done that, but when the McCalls bought me my first cell phone, they entered their names and numbers into the contacts. I never had a reason to memorize it. All I had to do was bring up either 'Mom' or 'Dad' in my contacts. God, I wished I would have been more aware of the importance.

After I placed the finger sandwiches on a plate and a small bowl of beef barley soup on a serving tray, I carried the tray with Rui's lunch to the study. The door was wide open, so I entered without knocking. Carefully setting the tray down on the low rectangular table between the two couches, I made my escape before he could yell at me for being late with his lunch or curse me because his soup was too hot or not hot enough.

In a sense, it was a good thing that most of the staff returned to the mansion. I could occupy my time with them instead of thinking about why I was here in the first place. Mostly it kept my mind off of Davian. In another way, it wasn't so good. There were too many staff members milling around the house to retrieve the cell phone I had taken from Rui's study. I needed to hang on for a little while longer. Tomorrow was Wednesday, and I knew Rui would go out of town. As long as I remained out of his way, I could avoid his wrath.

Every day since I arrived, I filled my mind with thoughts of Davian and how much I missed his warm touch, the way he held me at night. Thinking about him gave me the strength I needed and a reason to keep fighting. I had to keep my head up. It would be only a matter of time until Davian would come to rescue me from this monster. I was sure of it.

After waiting an hour, I went to the study to remove the lunch tray. I put it off longer than I should have, but only because I wanted to avoid a confrontation with Rui.

When I entered his office, he was sitting in his chair with his back was toward the door. His focus was on the window behind his desk. I wasn't sure what he was looking at, but I was thankful that it wasn't me. Quietly, I picked up the tray and turned to head out of the study. When his deep voice echoed off the walls, I stopped my movements. "Do you know what they say about young women who sneak around, Reyna?"

My heart fell into my stomach, and I could feel my hands shaking as I held onto the tray. "I wasn't intentionally sneaking around, Rui. I just didn't want to disturb your thoughts."

When he spun his chair so he was facing me, there was a darkness in his eyes I knew all too well. He pushed from his chair and sauntered over to where I was standing. His breath smelled of alcohol as he leaned in and placed his mouth close to my ear. My body trembled with fear— punishment was soon to follow. "From now on, you will address me when you enter and when you leave. I think 'darling' would be appropriate, unless there is another name of endearment you would rather use."

The bile churning in my throat was making itself known. "Darling" wasn't the name that crossed my mind, but if it meant I would avoid punishment, I would do as he asked. "Yes, darling. Whatever you say."

Before I could make my escape, Rui pressed his lips to mine. He really could use some lessons on kissing. Not that it would matter. Just the thought of him touching me made sick.

Without another word, Rui walked back to his desk and took a seat in his chair. He spun his chair around and focused on the window. Waving his hand in the air, he said, "Go. I would like to be left alone with my thoughts."

His thoughts. Was he kidding? What could he possibly have to think about? Maybe the fact that he was holding me against my will. Perhaps that what he was doing was wrong. Or maybe what his next move would be to control me even further.

Once I rinsed off the plates, I placed them inside the dishwasher. Helga, one of the staff members, entered the kitchen. Evidently, she could tell I was unhappy by the way I was rinsing off the dishes. "You know if you break the dishes, you will make Mr. Salko furious."

"Let him be angry. I don't care." My anger boiled over and spilled onto her. Her body became small, and she turned to leave the kitchen with her head lowered. "Wait, I'm sorry. I didn't mean to yell at you."

Helga stopped and turned around. "I know. Mr. Salko brings out the worst in people." Helga smiled, and it was nice to see, even if for a short while.

"Please, sit and chat with me." I wasn't really close to any of the staff, but Helga was closer to me than the others. She helped me become a better cook and never judged me when I did something wrong. Maybe she could become a friend. It was clear that she had also seen Rui's temper.

"Only for a moment," she agreed, taking a seat at the kitchen table.

Pulling out the chair next to her, I placed my hands on the table. "Can you tell me how long you have been working for Mr. Salko?"

"I've been under his employment for a while." She paused for a moment, her hands now settling under the table on her lap. "It's so nice to have another Mrs. Salko in the house. It has been a long time."

"Rui was married before? What happened to her?" I wasn't sure why it surprised me. It seemed logical that he was.

"She died suddenly. About sixteen years ago. She was so kind and beautiful. You remind me of her. You two could have been sisters."

"How did she die?"

"Mr. Salko never spoke of it, but from what I gather, she went quickly." Helga's voice cracked, her emotions getting the best of her.

"It is sad when someone is taken so quickly because of a terminal illness," I said, feeling her pain.

"Oh, no, Mrs. Salko. Anya didn't die from an illness. She was in a car accident."

My head was spinning. There were so many things wrong with this conversation. Anya Salko was Rui's wife's name, the same name that appeared on my fake passport. She died in a car accident, just like my mom had. And even stranger yet, Helga mentioned that we could have been sisters. This conversation made me more interested in Anya Salko. "Can you tell me more about the previous Mrs. Salko?"

"I could talk about her all day, but unfortunately, I have work to do. Mr. Salko doesn't like his staff to get lazy. Maybe when I finish my duties, we will have a chance to chat more."

Helga stood from her chair and left the kitchen, leaving me to my thoughts. Questions were whirling around in my head like a tornado. The day Rui took me, he admitted having a relationship with my mother, but he never mentioned them being married. Anya and my mom had to be two different people. They had to be, especially since Lorenzo stated that my mom hated him. There was no way my mom would ever marry Rui. He was a monster. Why didn't I look more closely at the passport that Rui showed me? The picture could have been of my mom and not me.

After my conversation with Helga, the remainder of the day was a complete blur. I still had an hour before I needed to head back downstairs to cook Rui dinner. Helga must have been busy with her own duties since I didn't see her after our conversation. The cell phone I had taken from Rui's study was still in the drawer, and if I didn't get it soon, someone would find it. I wasn't sure if it was even still there. Surely if it wasn't and someone had found it, I would have heard about it from Rui. The best chance of getting it would be when Rui had gone to bed. Besides kissing me, Rui had made no other advances toward me. I was confident that he would sleep in his room and never come to mine. Until I could call Kenzi, I needed to remain patient.

Pushing from my bed, I headed down the steps to prepare dinner for Rui. Earlier I had taken two lamb chops from the freezer to thaw. Helga showed me a great lamb recipe and informed me it was Rui's favorite. I didn't really care that it was, but the last thing I wanted was to get punished for cooking him something he wouldn't consider worth eating.

When I reached the bottom of the steps, I could hear Rui yelling in Russian. Whoever he was talking to had pissed him off. I was glad that it wasn't me, but then again, it meant his anger would be taken out on me. All the more reason to avoid him. As I walked past his study to the kitchen, my name slipped from his mouth. "Reyna."

Just the sound of my name off his tongue made my skin crawl. Clenching my fists, I turned on my heels and walked into his study. I remembered what he had said earlier. Using all the strength I had, I said, "Yes, darling."

I could have puked right then and then. The same cold eyes that I had been victim to since he brought me here were on me. "It seems that you have been putting your nose where it doesn't belong."

The conversation I had with Helga. Crap! Somehow, he found out about it. I had to think of something fast. "If you are referring to the conversation I had with Helga, then yes, I inquired about you. But you have to understand, darling. It was only so I could do more to please you. I was trying to find out what you like and what you don't."

Placing my hand on his cheek, I did the one thing I thought I would never do. I stood on my toes and placed my lips on his. *God, forgive me.*

~4~

Davian

Patton and I pulled up to the old house where Reyna used to live. From what we had learned, the house hadn't been lived in for sixteen years. It was evident that someone was taking care of the upkeep. The lawn was green, and the shrubs were perfectly manicured. The house was also very well maintained. Someone owned the house, or at the very least, was taking care of it.

As we got out of the SUV, Patton and I looked at each other, noticing a blue truck parked across the street in front of the house. Patton pulled his phone from his back pocket and took a picture of the license plate. The truck parked across the street might be just that, or it could be there for a reason. Wouldn't it be ironic if it belonged to Giles Curtis?

The house looked quiet, and there was no sign that anyone was around when we walked up the six steps to the house. I continued to look around, wondering why this place was so important to keep up. There wasn't anything special about it. Just like the other homes in the neighborhood, the house was old, with a porch that extended the length of the front of the house. An old wooden swing hung on one side of the porch with a rocker a few feet away. I could picture Reyna sitting on the swing playing dolls or Louise reading her book.

Patton reached the front door first and cupped his hands against the side window next to the door. "I don't see any movement inside."

We were at the right place. It was the address that Curtis had given me. There was no doorbell, so I tapped my fist against the door. We were almost ready to give up and head to the back of the house when the door opened. A bald man, about six feet tall with a large build, stood before us. He looked familiar, and I knew it was Giles Curtis. He was five years older, but hadn't changed. My eyes fell to his waist, and I could see he wasn't packing. "Why don't you two come in? We have a lot to discuss."

Curtis stepped to the side and allowed us to enter. As I looked around, the home appeared updated. It looked lived in and very well kept. Curtis closed the door behind us and said, "We can talk in the living room."

The way things were going was far from what I expected. I had prepared myself for an altercation. Patton and I took a seat on the couch, while Curtis took a seat on the chair across from us.

The scene before me was making me uncomfortable. Curtis was too calm. "I don't know what your game is, Curtis, but I want some answers."

"Please call me Brax. I'll tell you everything I know."

I was just about to lay into him when an older woman appeared in the doorway. I couldn't take my eyes off her. She seemed familiar to me. Then it hit me. If I hadn't known better, she could have been the woman in the photo that Reyna carried around her neck. But Louise Braxton died sixteen years ago, so it wasn't possible. It had to be a sister or a cousin.

"Hey, Brax, do you want me to bring in some tea or anything else to drink?" she said in a soft voice.

"No, thank you," I said before he could answer. "Have we met?"

She looked over to Brax, waiting for some kind of approval before she answered my question. "It's okay, Lou. Why don't you join us? This conversation includes you."

My head was spinning. What the hell was going on? The authorities proved that Louise Braxton died when her car went over the cliff on Suches Loop. No one could fake dental records. It was the only thing left of her remains that confirmed her identity. As I watched Louise take a seat next to Brax, I couldn't help but notice how her movements were so much like Reyna's. It must have been my imagination, but everything about her reminded me of Reyna. Her hair, her eyes, her petite frame. Everything.

It was driving me crazy. I needed answers. "Are you Louise Braxton?"

Once again, she looked to Brax for approval. When he nodded his head, she looked at me. "I am. Can you tell me about my daughter?"

Fuck! What the hell was I supposed to say to that? "Before I answer your question, how the fuck is this even possible? The authorities confirmed your death."

"Maybe if I start from the beginning," Curtis interjected. "It will answer a lot of your questions. I hope you don't have immediate plans. This could take a while."

"By all means." Sarcasm wasn't my thing, but I was growing more impatient by the minute.

Curtis scooted forward in his chair, his elbows resting on his knees. He seemed relaxed as he began. "As you probably already know, I worked for Rui Salko. He considered me his right-hand man. I pretty much did all the dirty work for him." Curtis emphasized the word "dirty" by using his fingers to create quotation marks.

"Your relationship with Rui Salko is no secret, Curtis," I said. "What I want to know is how the hell Louise Braxton is sitting here instead of inside an unclaimed container on a shelf somewhere?"

"I'm getting to that." Curtis glared in annoyance as he ran his hand along his bald head. A sign of nervousness becoming more evident.

Before he could continue, Louise placed her hand on his knee and said, "Rui and I were married. I'm not sure if it was even legal."

"It's okay, Lou. I'll take it from here." Curtis chimed in as Louise's emotions kicked in. "I knew what kind of man Rui Salko was and how badly he treated her. I couldn't stand it. I hated what he did to her. It had to stop, and I had to stop it." Curtis stood, and I swore I could see the steam rolling off his bald head. Gathering his composure, he took a seat next to Louise and gave her a sympathetic smile. "To this day, I'm not sure how it happened, but Lou and I fell in love. I had to get her away from him. So, when the time was right, I did just that."

"So, you faked her death." I was on my feet, pacing the length of the small living room. Dropping my gaze to Curtis, I met his eyes. "Who was in the car?"

"I'll get to that. We hadn't planned on a fake death, not at first, but eventually, I had to. Rui found out where she was. And in order to keep our secret, faking her death was the only way out. If he found out that I had anything to do with her disappearance, he would have killed me. I continued to work for that motherfucker so he would never question her death or my relationship with Lou. I've waited sixteen years to be out from under his bullshit. Just waiting until we could finally be together again. You could say it was a way out for both of us."

It was a nice story, but still left unanswered questions. "You still haven't answered my question about who was in the car. And how was the body identified as Louise Braxton's?"

"I used my connections and got my hands on a cadaver from the university. Anyone can be bought with the right amount of money." Curtis's jaw set in a hard line when he looked at me. "As you might have guessed, time was something we didn't have much of."

"How does your sister fit into all of this?" My mind was still digesting the fact that Louise was still alive, and Reyna lived her childhood without her mother. They all knew, even Margaret knew.

"She was our eyes and ears until the McCalls stepped in. We hadn't planned on Reyna being adopted, but not even my sister could stop it. All we have ever wanted was to keep Reyna safe. We thought if Reyna was moved from foster house to foster house, it would be harder for Rui to find her. Disappearing without a word five years ago was a mistake, and I can't take it back, but being without Lou would have been even worse."

The pieces were falling into place. I had a hand in Reyna's adoption. Just like Curtis, we knew Salko would eventually come out of the woodwork. All this time, Salko knew Reyna wasn't his daughter. But how? He took her for one reason, which was to draw out Curtis. Funny how things worked. We were using Reyna for the same reason, to fish out Salko. But the minute I laid eyes on Reyna I couldn't exchange her life for his. All I wanted was to protect her. I failed. Just like I failed Gwen.

I considered what Curtis just confessed, and no matter the facts, I wanted Salko dead. Something still bothered me. Call it intuition or logic. Either way, I had to hear it from Curtis. "Are you Reyna's father, or is Salko?"

Looking at Louise, Curtis smiled, and I knew. "Reyna is our daughter."

"Then tell me one thing. How you did it? We proved through DNA testing Salko was Reyna's father. We had a sample of his blood."

The room became deathly quiet. We were all looking at each other for answers, but the only person who knew the truth was Curtis. "I switched the blood samples," he blurted. "I knew something was up when the new guy took a sample of Rui's blood. There was a reason he wanted his blood, and I couldn't chance Rui blaming me for whatever the hell that sample was going to be used for. I needed him to trust me. Underneath my disgust for the man, he was my boss, and my loyalty had to remain with him." Curtis paused for a moment with a chuckle. "It's a funny thing. Soon after the altercation that got Rui shot, the new guy disappeared." His eyes opened wide as though a light went on that was turned off for five years. Shaking his head back and forth, he looked over to me. "He was one of yours?"

"How could you be loyal to a man like that? After what he did to Louise. You, of all people, knew what kind of man he was and still is. For God's sake, you took his wife." I looked at him, repulsed, avoiding the obvious.

"As I said, I had to remain loyal to him. As far as he knew, Louise was dead, and I wanted to keep it that way until I could break my ties with him. And for the record, Lou's marriage to Salko wasn't legal."

There was some truth in what Curtis said. He took Louise from Salko to save her. Faking her death was the only way they could ensure that Salko wouldn't look for her. If Salko found out that Louise was still alive, he wouldn't hesitate to kill her. If he ever found them, I was certain Louise would die a slow death, and Salko would make sure Curtis watched her suffer before the same slow death was bestowed on him.

Even though the pieces were falling into place, there was the issue concerning the letter found in Louise's safe deposit box. "What about the letter?"

Curtis and Louise either didn't know about it or were surprised that we had found it. Curtis's expression was off when he met my gaze. "It's fake."

He was lying. Patton and I knew it. Guilt was plastered all over his face. "I don't believe you, Curtis. There is something else to this story you aren't telling us."

"I don't care what you believe. All I know is that Salko has our daughter, and we will not stop looking for her. I've had to wait sixteen years to be with Louise. I'm not waiting for another sixteen to be with my daughter. It would be better for us to work together on this instead of against each other. Either you're with me or you're not."

I was ready to ask him about his men camped out in front of The Regency, but decided to save that question for another time. It was clear he was concerned about Reyna's safety as much as I was. Maybe he could help us. It was better to keep him close. Curtis might not be my enemy, but I didn't trust him.

When we left the house, Patton and I headed out to Suches Loop, where the staged accident happened. It was probably it was a waste of time, but I still wanted to check it out. As we drove further up the loop, we saw that just like the reviews on the road indicated, it was treacherous. Personally, I would think twice about driving this road at night. While Patton drove, I got the chance to look around. An accident that happened sixteen years ago wouldn't leave much behind, but we got lucky. The stretch of road where the car went through the guardrail was still visible, but only because the repaired section was less weathered. I was certain we were at the right place since there were no other spots along the road that stuck out. I wished I had asked Curtis exactly where it was Louise supposedly went over the edge.

Patton slowed down and pulled over to the side of the road to avoid getting hit by oncoming traffic. When I opened my door, I realized just how close he had parked to the railing. I carefully got out of the SUV, accidentally hitting the door against the guardrail. The SUV was dangerously close to the edge of the cliff. As I looked over the railing, I knew no one would have survived a fall over the edge. The drop-off was steep with rugged terrain. Not even the trees or vegetation would have helped break the fall.

Sixteen years was a long time, and any evidence of Louise's car flying over the edge was long gone. Searching for clues here was a mistake and a waste of time, like my father said. Curtis admitted staging Louise's death to keep her safe. And to think, all this time I blamed Salko for her death. Still, my gut told me something was still missing. What caused Curtis to leave Salko's employment, other than how he treated women, and what was he hiding beside Louise?

~5~

Reyna

As the days passed, I saw very little of Helga. Rui had remained at home, never leaving his study except to have his breakfast, which he continued to enjoy in the garden with me by his side. I still hadn't been able to retrieve the cell phone from the accent table. The longer I waited, the more I risked getting caught.

If I wanted to get out of here, I had to stay on his good side. I didn't know how long it would be until Rui made a move to consummate our fake marriage, but I felt like my time was running out. The bright side to this madness was that I gained his trust by doing exactly what he asked, which included calling him "darling" when I addressed him. It appeared I was doing more right than wrong, trying hard to avoid his wrath. The only thing that kept me going was Davian. It seemed like a lifetime ago that we were together. Thoughts of Davian were the only things that gave me the strength to survive until rescued.

After breakfast, Rui went to his study while I

cleaned up the breakfast dishes. Once again, I made more than we could eat and ended up putting the leftovers down the disposal. I tried to get the portions correct, but I found it challenging to cook for two people. Dinner portions were the easiest to prepare. They were mostly composed of one meat and two vegetables, per Rui's request. And, of course, his insistence on having a salad.

When I placed the last plate in the dishwasher, I filled the soap dispenser with detergent and turned it on. After I wiped down the last of the counters, there was plenty of time before Rui would need me, so I headed out the back door to enjoy the garden. I took in the beautiful morning and walked down the brick path toward the garden. There was a slight chill in the air, and soon the leaves on the trees would turn colors. Of all the seasons, Fall was my favorite. Hopefully, before the leaves fell, Davian and I would be together to enjoy them, along with the Thanksgiving holiday. These were the thoughts that kept me strong. I had to remain positive. At the very least, I should be thankful that Rui trusted me enough to allow me to wander around the grounds.

Other than the birds carrying on an exclusive conversation with each other, the garden was quiet. Walking in the garden was the only escape I had, even if it was for a short time. *How could a man so evil create a garden so beautiful and comforting?* There was no way he could. Just then, the thought of Anya Salko came to mind. If she was as Helga described her, I had a feeling she had something to do with creating such a beautiful garden.

Lost in my thoughts, I reached the bench where I usually sat to admire the small pond bordered by impatiens flowers in an assortment of colors. There was a fountain that sprayed up in the shape of an umbrella in the middle of the pond. The sound of the water was so soothing, and I felt like I could enter a different place—a place where only Davian and I existed. Closing my eyes, I allowed the sound of the water to take me back to him.

"I love you, my sweet Reyna. I will forever worship you."

Davian's hand reached for mine. His touch was gentle as he brought my hand to his lips. Never once did he pull his eyes from mine. His lips were on mine, and I melted into his warmth. As though I weighed nothing at all, he scooped me into his arms and placed me on the soft grass. He hovered above me for a moment before placing his mouth over mine.

There was no one else, just us together, just as we belonged. Caressing my cheek, Davian looked down at me, and his eyes said more than I could comprehend. The tenderness was overwhelming. This wasn't how it was supposed to be. I belonged to him. We belonged together.

The chance of never seeing Davian again tore me apart. My heart hurt, and I couldn't stop the tears from falling. I swore I wouldn't shed another tear for Rui Salko, but I was afraid that this would be my life. I would rather die than live under his control.

I needed to stop and have faith. Davian wouldn't leave me here. He knew what kind of man Rui Salko was. Shaking the negative thoughts away, I noticed something along the six-foot hedge I hadn't seen before. It was shiny. Pushing to my feet, I walked over to the tall shrubs. I moved the branches out of the way the best that I could, but the hedge was too thick to make out what it was. If only I had something to trim the branches. Shears would be great to have right now. Determined, I continued to move the branches, knowing my arms were getting scraped.

When I finally could see between the leaves, a gate appeared on the other side. I thought it was strange that a gate would be hidden behind the hedge. The area I had cleared was too small for me to squeeze through. As much as I wanted to find out what was behind the gate, I needed to head back to the house. I spent far too long in the garden, and soon Rui would demand his lunch. Tomorrow, I would come back better prepared. Maybe I found my escape.

When I returned to the house, I found Rui in one of his moods. Something must have happened while I was gone to cause him to be so angry. Thankfully, I wasn't the person taking the brunt of his anger. One of Rui's staff left his study with his head hung low. I didn't know what had taken place, but I knew Rui's temper all too well and felt sorry for the young man. The best thing for me was to avoid him, head to the kitchen, and attempt to make him a lunch he would never forget.

Despite a perfect lunch displayed on the serving tray that I spent the better of an hour preparing, I was snubbed when I reached his office. "You shouldn't have wasted your time, Reyna. After the day I've had, I need to get out of here."

I didn't dare ask if I should save it for later. Instead, I nodded my head and left his study with the tray. I hadn't made it to the kitchen when I heard the door slam behind me. He was gone, and my chance to get the cell phone from the accent table had finally come. I hurried to the kitchen and placed the tray of food on the counter.

As I pulled the drawer open, I held my breath. My eyes fell on the small flip phone and the charger. My lungs deflated as I let out the breath I held in. Grabbing the phone as quickly as I could, I ran up the stairs and entered my room. Now that I had the phone, I had no idea what to do with it. I had to charge it, but where? I couldn't risk Rui or one of his staff finding it. I looked around the room. There had to be an outlet near the bed since a lamp sat on the nightstand. Closing the bedroom door, I walked over to the bed and searched for the outlet.

The outlet was just behind the headboard and was hard to access. Once I plugged the charger in the outlet, I pulled the cord down the headboard near the bed frame and hid the wire behind the bed. Unless someone was looking for it, it wasn't visible. Plugging the phone into the charger, I flipped the phone open to make sure it was charging. The battery symbol read only 2%, but as the bar began moving up and down, I knew it was charging. Before I slid it between the upper and lower mattress near the head of the bed, I brought the phone to life and placed it on silent. I only prayed that it would charge quickly, and I could call Kenzi before Rui got home.

Before I could head downstairs, I needed a few moments to calm down. My heart was racing, and I needed to slow it down. I took a lungful of air, in and out, until I could feel my heart beating regularly. *I did it*. I was one step closer to getting out of this place.

With my composure intact, I opened the door to my room. Two stone-cold eyes met mine. I was speechless, but knew I had to remain calm. "You scared me, darling. Did you decide to have lunch? Would you like me to warm it for you?"

"I have something much more important to deal with than lunch. Where is it, Reyna?"

My chest tightened, and I knew he had caught me. Playing dumb, I took a step closer to where he was still standing in the doorway. "Where is what, darling?"

Rui's eyes remained on mine as he pulled his cell from his pocket. His teeth clenched as he used his index finger to punch numbers on the keyboard. Fear rippled through my body, the hope of ever getting out of here sinking out of sight like quicksand. All I could do was wait and pray that the flip phone I hid between the mattresses would remain silent.

Rui placed his cell to his ear, but only his footsteps sounded as he stormed through the bathroom door. Waiting for a moment, he turned to face me; his expression conveyed the fury inside him. It only took him two steps to be close enough to take hold of my arm. "I will only ask once, Reyna, where is the fucking phone?"

Only two choices were running through my mind. Lie or tell the truth. The phone didn't ring, so either the silent mode I put it on worked or it hadn't charged enough. Either way, I knew he would punish me. So, I lied. "I don't know what you're talking about. What phone? You took the only phone I had back in Atlanta."

Rui took his hand from my arm, but only to use it to strike me across the face. Dots flickered before my eyes as I tried my best to remain standing. My efforts failed, and I couldn't keep myself from falling. The pain radiating down my cheek was the worst yet.

Unable to move, I watched with one eye opened as Rui move through the room, dialing the number over and over. If he continued, it was only in a matter of time until he found it. Never had he been so angry, but I had to remain quiet. That phone was my only way out of here.

After several more tries, Rui finally gave up and slipped his cell inside his suit coat. The breath I had been holding drained from my lungs when he walked to the door and pulled it shut. If I lingered in the bedroom much longer, he would know I was hiding something from him. I waited this long; I could wait a while longer to call Kenzi. Pushing to my feet, I refrained from going to the bathroom to examine the damage he had done to my cheek. Placing my hand on the doorknob, I pulled it open. Rui was gone, but not from the house, I was sure of it. I got lucky this time, but next time I might not. I had to get out of here before he killed me.

~6~

Reyna

Shortly after my altercation with Rui, he left again. I couldn't keep the cell phone hidden forever. If anything, he was persistent, and eventually, he would find it. Thankfully, when Rui left the house, I was downstairs to divert any suspicions he might have had about the phone.

Waiting a few moments, I looked out the window to see Rui's car in the distance. When I could no longer see his car, I hurried to clean the kitchen before going back upstairs. The lunch that I had prepared for him ended up in the trash.

When I reached my room, I looked out the window again to make sure he wasn't on his way back. I couldn't risk him coming back before I could make a call to Kenzi.

Pulling the phone from between the two mattresses, I flipped it open to find that I had plenty of battery life to make a quick call. I dialed Kenzi's number while keeping my eyes on the road leading from the mansion.

"Hello," Kenzi answered hesitantly.

"Kenzi, I only have a few minutes. I am somewhere in Toronto, Ontario, in the country. Rui Salko took me." My eyes were on the road as I spoke.

"Oh my God, Reyna, are you okay? We have been so worried about you. Davian has been going nuts trying to find you." Worry was in her voice, and I wished I could reassure her I was okay when, in reality, I was far from it.

"I'm okay." I lied. "Please tell Davian where I am and that I am okay. Please don't call me back. I can't risk getting caught with this phone. I have to go. I will try to call again."

"Wait."

There was so much more I wanted to say, but instead, I ended the call before I got caught. I might not get another chance to call her back, but hopefully, the information I gave her was enough for Davian and his men to find me. I made sure the ringer was off before I tucked the phone back between the mattresses. The emotional turmoil building finally let loose, and the tears fell one right after the other. So many emotions gathered inside my head. *Fear. Excitement. Hope.* With every one of them, I was confident that Davian would find me and rescue me from this horrible nightmare.

A knock at the door pulled me from my unpreventable breakdown. Wiping away the remaining tears from my face, I stood and walked to the door. When I pulled it open, Helga was standing on the other side. Her shoulders were drawn together, and her expression was slack. As I got closer, I saw the redness in her eyes, which confirmed that she had been crying.

"What's wrong?" I asked, placing my hand on her shoulder.

Helga moved her head back and forth, and tears fell down her cheeks. Pulling her inside my room, I took a quick scan of the hallway before closing the door. As we sat on the bed, I could tell that she needed to get whatever upset her off her chest. "What has you so upset, Helga? Whatever it is, it can't be so bad that we can't figure something out together."

"Oh, Mrs. Salko. It is something no one can fix." Helga's tears were real and her voice cracked with emotion.

"Tell me what it is. Maybe I can help."

Sucking in a breath, Helga's eyes met mine. "I'm afraid you won't ever return. Mr. Salko has made arrangements for you and him to leave." Heartbreak and helplessness filled her eyes as she continued to sob.

"What arrangements?"

"After Anya…" Helga hesitated, correcting herself. "I mean, Mrs. Salko. After Mrs. Salko died, there have been other women brought to the mansion by Mr. Salko. At first, I thought it was to replace the loss of Mrs. Salko, but when Mr. Salko commanded me to prepare them for the arrangements he had made, the women never returned to the mansion."

"How many women, Helga? How long have you been here?" My mind was spinning with the realization of what Helga was implying.

"I was only thirteen when I came to live with Mr. Salko. The first two years weren't too bad, but then when I turned fifteen, things changed. He expected more of me. He had needs, desires."

I could feel the breakfast from hours ago make its way up my throat. It didn't take a genius to know what Helga was talking about. Rui used her for his sexual needs. Her being here wasn't of her own free will. Just like me, he took her. "Helga, did Mr. Salko kidnap you?"

"No, no. Mrs. Salko. Mr. Salko saved me. He offered to provide me a place to sleep. He gave me food. He made sure I had nice clothes. As long as I did as he asked, he would take care of me."

I couldn't believe what I was hearing. I knew human trafficking was out there, but never in my wildest dreams did I ever think I would be faced with it. "Helga, how old are you?"

"I think I am twenty-nine. I haven't celebrated a birthday since coming here."

If she was right, that would make her eight years older than me. For sixteen years, she had endured that monster. Unable to hold down the bile that was creeping up my throat, I pushed from the bed and hurried to the bathroom. I held my hand over my mouth until I was safely kneeling before the toilet. The contents of my stomach filled the porcelain bowl. The sight of Helga being mauled and molested by Rui contaminated my mind—the picture of a young woman screaming for her life playing over and over.

A gentle hand came down on my back. "Mrs. Salko, are you okay?"

Using the back of my hand, I rubbed it across my mouth and pushed to my feet. Helga watched me without saying a word as I turned the faucet on and brought a hand full of water to my mouth. Swishing the water against my teeth a few times, I spit it in the sink. There wasn't anything I could say to Helga. I only stared back at her through the reflection of the mirror.

Removing a hand towel from the counter, I wiped my mouth before facing her. "I'm sorry for everything he has done to you." I began. "Helga, haven't you ever tried to escape?"

Lowering her head, she said, "Where would I go?"

I felt like I could trust her, but not enough to tell her that help was on the way. She didn't deserve what Rui had done to her, but I felt like her loyalty was to him. Raising her chin, I met her eyes. "Is this what you were trying to tell me?"

"We need to hurry." Helga avoided my question. "Mr. Salko left to meet with one of them. He will be back soon. I need to help you prepare."

"Prepare for what, Helga?"

"To leave for the arrangement Mr. Salko has made. Mr. Salko wanted to make sure you looked your best. That is why I am here. I am to help you."

"Where is he going to take me, Helga?"

"Mr. Salko never tells us where. He only tells us when arrangements have been made."

If I hadn't already spilled everything from my stomach, I would have thrown up. No wonder Rui hadn't touched me. There was only one reason the previous women he brought to the mansion never returned from his so-called arrangement. They were merchandise. I was his merchandise and that was the reason he abstained from touching me. It was clear. The way Helga looked when I opened the door confirmed his intention. Just like the other women, she was a prisoner with nowhere to go. She probably felt like there was no other choice but to live with the torture Rui had put her through.

I was an excellent judge of people's expressions and could tell whether they were lying or telling the truth. Taking Helga by the hand, I focused on her face. I asked the one question I hoped I wouldn't later regret. "If you had the chance to leave the mansion and be free of Mr. Salko, would you try to escape?"

There was no hesitation as her lips trembled with fear. "Yes."

I wasn't ready to tell Helga of my plan or the fact that I had contacted Kenzi. I couldn't risk her telling Rui that I had a phone. Although her actions seemed sincere, I needed to wait a little longer to tell her of my plan. I had to be sure that she wouldn't run to Rui with the information I shared with her. "I can only tell you, don't give up hope."

Smiling, she squeezed my hand and walked away from me to the bedroom. "We better get you ready."

I watched Helga walk inside the closet. Whatever she chose for me wouldn't make a rat's ass bit of difference. Soon Davian would rescue me from this place, and also

Helga. Hell would have to freeze over before I would ever agree to Rui's business exchange.

I stood just outside the closet doorway while Helga slid the hangers over one by one until she found the perfect outfit. Facing me, she held it up for me to inspect. "I think this will look quite nice on you."

I walked over to her and took the dress and placed it back on the rack. "What I am wearing is fine. There is no way I am going to allow Rui to sell me."

"Please, Reyna, you must do as he asked."

That was the first time Helga had ever addressed me by using my first name. "What difference does it make how I look? I will not allow Rui to use me as merchandise."

"Because if you don't, he will make my life here unbearable."

Helga reached for the floral dress and handed it to me with shaky hands. She was afraid and falling victim to Rui's discipline. I feared she would receive the worst of it if I didn't do as she asked. Hesitantly, I took the dress from her hand. With one last-ditch effort, I asked, "What would it take for me to stay here instead of leaving the mansion?"

~7~

Davian

Heading out to Suches Loop ended up being a dead end. Too many years had passed, and whatever remained of Louise's so-called accident was long gone. Still, I had to wonder what Curtis meant by the letter being a fake. Musing while pulling my email up from my phone, I knew I missed something, and the letter was the key to everything. It was possibly the only way to find out where Salko had taken Reyna.

Hitting the attachment that Patton sent me in the email, I opened it up and waited for it to load. When the letter appeared, I reread it. One sentence stuck out. *"Never look back, only forward. Your pot of gold will be waiting for you to take."* If the letter was a fake, as Curtis confessed, then why include this phrase?

Another visit with Curtis was in order. Patton's eyes were on the road, but I could tell that he was wondering what was going through my head. Glancing my way, he asked, "What's going on in that head of yours?"

"I think Curtis is a fucking liar. There is no way this

letter can be fake. I was going to let it slide, but I think it's time he tells us the truth."

Patton was an open book. The way he shook his head exhibited his annoyance. "Care to elaborate?"

"It's just a hunch, but I think Curtis did more than take Louise from Rui. I think he took something more valuable than his precious wife."

"And you got all of that from the letter?"

Maybe I was reaching, but there was only one way to find out. "We'll soon find out."

Patton parked in front of the house, and we both got out. The blue truck parked across the street in front of Reyna's childhood home was gone. We hadn't heard from Axe on the plate either. There was no way of knowing whether or not the truck belonged to Curtis. When we reached the front door, I knew something was off. Even though it was a quiet subdivision in a small town, and most residents kept to themselves with their only worry being to keep their lawns groomed and their flowers watered, leaving a door wide open didn't sit well with me.

Since I was unarmed, Patton took the lead. Pulling his gun from his holster, he entered the house first. The inside wasn't the same as when we previously arrived. Whoever paid them a visit sliced the furniture with a knife and pulled the stuffing out. It appeared they were looking for something and didn't care what they destroyed to find it. As we headed upstairs, it was the same scene. All the rooms were taken apart—the mattresses sliced just like the furniture in the living room. Looking at the empty drawers that were still hanging open, it appeared that Louise and Curtis left in a hurry. There were no clothes inside or scattered around.

Digging my phone out of my pocket, I searched my contacts for Curtis's number. I had added it from Margaret's phone. After the fourth ring, the call went to voice mail. Instead of trying again, I sent him a quick text. *Where the fuck are you?*

Only one other person would know where Curtis would go, and that was Margaret. She proved to be a resourceful woman, and it wouldn't surprise me if she figured out a way to get in touch with him even without her cell phone. Margaret Curtis was worth visiting before we headed back to the warehouse.

A Ford Escape was parked in front of her double-wide trailer, which told us that Margaret was home. We walked up the wooden steps, which announced our arrival as they creaked like they desperately needed replacing. Before my knuckles met the aluminum screen door, Margaret pulled open the door. "What the hell do you want?"

Pulling her cell from my pocket, I held it up,

offering it back to her. "Tell me where your brother is."

In a matter of seconds, Margaret swung the screen door open and grabbed her cell from my grip. I had no use for it since I had entered her brother's number on my phone, and Axe was already tracking it from the warehouse. If Margaret made a move, we would know. As long as she did nothing stupid like turn her phone off, we would know exactly where she went.

"I don't know where my brother is." Her eyes shifted between us, scrutinizing our presence.

"I think you do. If you don't let us know where your brother is, you're putting Louise and him in danger." I knew mentioning Louise would get a response out of her.

"If you know about Louise, then you have already talked to Brax. You might as well come inside." The offer was strange, but she stepped out of the way to allow us to enter.

The smell of cigarettes still lingered in the air, which reminded me why I never indulged in the addictive habit. Patton and I remained standing close to the door while Margaret took a seat on the couch where a freshly lit cigarette was smoldering in a ceramic ashtray. Meeting us with her gaze, she took a long drag from the cigarette. "Brax was here about an hour ago. He said he had to leave the house in Gainesville. He said it was no longer safe."

"Did he tell you where they were going?" I asked, hoping that he told her where he was headed.

"Not the exact location. Only that they were heading back to Chicago. Brax said he had more connections there, and it would be safer there instead of in Georgia."

"Someone paid them a visit in Gainesville. They were looking for something. Do you know who?"

"Brax told me two men, large builds, driving a white van, were waiting outside the house. He got suspicious, so they grabbed what they could and left through the back door." Margaret inhaled another long drag from her cigarette, holding it between her index and middle finger. "Brax thought it might have been Salko's men."

With the information Margaret shared, going back to Chicago seemed like the only option we had to find Louise and Brax. As we headed out the door, I paused and turned to face Margaret. "If you hear from your brother, call me. I've programmed my number in your phone."

My hand was on the handle of the screen when Margaret's voice cracked behind me. "You're Davian Cross?"

As I turned to face her, her focus was on her cell. "I am."

When she lifted her head, an insolent expression washed over her face. "I heard about what happened to your fiancée. Such a shame."

If I hadn't known better, I would have thought she might have had something to do with Gwen's death. There wasn't a single ounce of compassion behind her heartless eyes. "What do you know about her death?"

"Nothing. Just what was in the papers."

Margaret was lying. "What happened to Gwen was withheld from the papers. How could you possibly know what happened to her?"

The only information publicized was her funeral's date and time, which was in small print and didn't stand out in the newspaper. Margaret's eyes clouded over as she stomped out her cigarette. "Don't be naïve, Mr. Cross. Now get out of my house."

A confrontation was senseless. She was our only tie to Brax Curtis. "Call me if you hear from your brother."

The information Margaret shared was questionable, and it was plain as day on Patton's face as he put the key in the ignition. "I think Margaret Curtis knows more than she is letting on."

"I have to agree with you, which is why we will keep tabs on her." I wasn't about to let her out of my sight. *Keep your enemies closer.*

Patton chose to go back to the warehouse to see what information he could find on Giles Curtis and his sister Margaret. I was beyond exhausted when Patton dropped me off at The Regency. Shortly after midnight, I got to my quiet penthouse after having a drink in the hotel bar. I had spent all of my time at the warehouse after Salko had taken Reyna since staying at the penthouse wasn't the same. I missed her like hell, and each day that passed, I feared it would bring me closer to losing her forever.

The smell of Margaret's ratty doublewide lingered between the fibers of my $3000 suit, and as tired as I was, I had to get rid of the stench that was clinging to my skin. Even though the hot blast of water washed away the stench, it did nothing to relieve the ache inside my gut. Reyna was my life, and without her here, I was nothing. The thought of never feeling her body next to mine, or the softness of her skin beneath my hands, ripped my heart in two. I had to find her. I had to get her back. I loved her.

I loved Reyna.

My beautiful Reyna.

Since Salko took Reyna, my ability to sleep was nonexistent. Almost four fucking weeks had passed with nothing. When I got my hands on that son-of-a-bitch, he would be a dead man. Grunting in frustration, I pushed from the couch and headed to my study. After Patton dropped me off last night, I remained here, trying to clear my head with no interruptions. If Patton needed me to go to the warehouse, he would let me know. With nothing to go on, I booted up my computer and stared at the monitor. The time was approaching 5:00 p.m., and I had no clue what I was looking for, but I had to do something. I lowered my eyes to my desk and Salko's folder met my gaze. I had gone through the information at least a hundred times, hoping there was something there I might have missed. After picking up the folder, my phone vibrated on my desk. It was shortly after 5:00 p.m., and my tension tripled when I flipped over my cell and saw Kenzi's number displayed across the screen.

Swiping the phone icon, I put the phone to my ear. "Kenzi, is everything okay?"

"Davian, oh, God. It's Reyna. She called me."

I wasn't sure if I heard Kenzi correctly. She had the tendency to be overly dramatic. "Calm down, Kenzi. Tell me again, who called you?"

I could hear her taking deep breaths, trying to calm herself as I suggested. "Reyna called me about five minutes ago. I don't know how, but she did. She said some man named Rui Salko had taken her to Toronto, Ontario. She didn't know where, but it was to a large mansion somewhere in the country."

I swore my heart stopped. Finally, after all this time, we got a break. "What's the number she called you from?"

"I don't know, Davian. The number came up restricted. I tried calling her back, but she never answered. There was no way to leave a message."

"I'll get in touch with Patton. He'll be able to retrieve the number."

"Davian…"

"Yeah…"

"She sounded really scared."

~8~

Davian

I was out the door before Kenzi hung up. Reyna was alive and in Toronto, Ontario. As the elevator descended to the parking garage, my first call was to Patton to tell him everything I could about the call with Kenzi.

Patience was a killer as I waited for him to pick up. "Patton, we got a break. Reyna called Kenzi. She is somewhere in Toronto, Ontario." Toronto was a large city, but not so large that we wouldn't find Reyna.

"Hold on." I heard Patton pounding his fingers against the keyboard before I hit the parking garage. Patton would never stop looking for answers, no matter how tired he was. His voice was scratchy when he finally spoke. "Nothing comes up in the public records in Toronto under Rui Salko. There are no hits on the companies he's affiliated with either, at least not on the ones we are already aware of. There are a few more places I can look. If the information we need is out there, I'll find it."

"I have faith in you. If anyone can locate her, you can. Meet me at the airport. We can revisit our search on the plane."

"You got it, boss. I'll let the others know so we are fully prepared once we land in Toronto."

Patton was resourceful, highly trained, and more than an asset to *The Society*. But even with the two of us, we would need more manpower to take down Salko once and for all. "Good. Have Sean stay with Kenzi in the event Reyna calls again."

"We'll find her, Davian." Hell yeah. We would find Reyna. Of that I was sure. Once she was safe, away from Salko, unharmed, I would have my revenge. By the time I finished with Rui Salko, he was going to wish he was dead.

Thirty minutes later, I pulled up to the hanger. Patton and Axe were loading the supplies we needed for our trip inside the aircraft's belly. I wasn't sure what would be waiting for us once we found Salko's country home or how many of Salko's men would be on the property. The last thing I wanted was to be unprepared.

Jeannie greeted me as I stepped on the plane. "Hello, Mr. Cross. Everything is ready for your flight to Canada. Calvin and Marcus are waiting in the conference room."

"Thank you, Jeannie. Do you know when we are

scheduled to take off? The sooner we are in the air, the better." Time was something I didn't have a lot of, especially where Reyna was concerned.

"Captain Matthews is getting the final okay from the tower. We should be taking off shortly. Can I get you anything before we take off?"

"Coffee. And lots of it."

Nodding her head, Jeannie headed to the small kitchen while I went to the conference room. Marcus and Calvin were seated at the table, already pounding their fingers against the keyboards of their laptops. Shortly after I took a seat at the table, Patton and Axe walked into the room.

Before Patton took a seat, he had his laptop open. "Let's see if I can find where you're hiding, Mr. Salko."

All eyes were on Patton as he pulled out a chair, placed his laptop on the table, and took a seat. As quickly as their eyes were on Patton, Marcus and Calvin were back typing on their computers, searching for any information regarding Salko's whereabouts.

Something about the way Patton looked at his computer screen had me concerned. I had worked with Patton a long time, enough to know that whenever he rubbed his fingers along his jawline, his brain was working overtime picking apart the information before him.

"I know that look, Patton. What do you have?"

"I don't know how we could have missed this, but Louise Braxton, aka Louise Murphy, is really Anya Salko. Look at this." Patton flipped his laptop around, allowing me to see what he had found.

I wasn't sure how we missed this either. Before me was a PDF document just like the birth certificate we found that proved Louise Braxton was Louise Murphy. "How is this possible? The birth certificate of Louise Murphy was recorded in the public records."

"I think someone with a lot of connections wanted to do whatever they had to, to keep her identity secret. The only person who knows her true identity for sure is Louise Braxton. Her identity is a concern, but look at the bottom of the document."

I scrolled down to the bottom of the document using the mouse pad until my eyes stopped on the witness' signature and relationship. There was no doubt that the signature belonged to Rui Salko. Besides his name, the word 'husband' was executed as the relationship. But, more importantly, was the address written below his name. It was in Toronto, Ontario, Canada. *Bingo.* Patton might have just found where Salko was holding Reyna.

My top priority was getting Reyna back. Dealing with Giles Curtis and Louise Braxton, and the fact that they lied, would need to wait. I hated being surprised, and it seemed as though with every bit of new information, more lies were being revealed. Un-fucking-believable.

Spinning Patton's laptop back towards him, I shook my head with disbelief. "I want everything you can find on Anya Salko. There has to be information on when she and Salko were married. Find out if they had children together, who their relatives are. I want to know the names of all the men working for that son-of-a-bitch and whatever else he might be into besides smuggling, trafficking, and extortion."

Patton's fingers began working against the keyboard as Marcus, Calvin, and Axe followed suit. With the four of them searching the dark web for information, I was confident that all the information on Salko would be found before we landed in Toronto.

Jeannie walked into the conference room with a pot of coffee and five cups. Not only did I lack sleep, but the other guys did too. Setting the tray in the center of the table, Jeannie looked over to us with a smile. "Is there anything else I can get you guys?"

In unison, we all looked over to Jeannie. "No, thank you."

Jeannie was part of the Cross family, just like the

rest of the guys. Even though she didn't serve, she was a survivor and had seen things no one should ever have to see—another victim of Rui Salko's unthinkable punishment tactics—like the women before her. Soon, his days of torturing women and children would be over, and so help me God, if he caused Reyna any harm, I would make sure he would die in the worst kind of hell possible.

Even with my growing concern for Reyna, I heard the dual Rolls-Royce engines of the jet came to life, which matched my cell's vibration on the conference table. Knowing there was only a brief window to answer the incoming call, I picked it off the table to find the caller unknown. I hesitated to answer the call, but remembered that Reyna called Kenzi from an unknown restricted number, and Patton found a way to forward this number from Kenzi's phone to mine. The timing couldn't have been any worse, but there was no way I was going to ignore this call. "Reyna."

"Davian?" My heart ripped into a thousand pieces when I heard her say my name.

"It's me, princess. We are on our way to Canada. We know where you are."

I wanted to hear sounds of joy from her lips, but only remorse echoed against my ear. "I'm so sorry I didn't listen to you. Rui Salko is a monster. He's not my father, Davian."

Even though my men were a few feet away, I felt alone and helpless. Knowing what Reyna was going through, regret took over, knowing I couldn't take her in my arms and make the pain go away. Until we touched down in Toronto, there wasn't a damn thing I could do for her other than give her hope. "Hang in there, princess. Just a little longer. Can you do that for me?"

"Hurry, Davian. Rui is taking me somewhere, and I'm afraid I'll never…"

The line went dead, and as much as I wanted to call her back, I couldn't risk her getting caught communicating with me. She was alone and scared, and based on her last comment my time was running out. *Damn.* If only we knew where Salko was taking her.

Not wasting any more time, I searched my contacts for Giles Curtis. He was my only hope in finding out where Salko would take Reyna. As the phone rang, my eyes fell to Patton, who was diligently typing on his keyboard. "Find out if there are any other properties that Salko owns in Canada. Reyna said he was taking her somewhere before the line went dead."

Patton heard my concern and said, "On it."

I wasn't sure what I was hoping for as I continued to stare at my phone. We were an hour away from touching down in Toronto and still clueless as to where Salko planned on taking Reyna. The thought that he might take her out of Canada had crossed my mind, but Salko wasn't stupid. Between my father's connection and mine, if he came back to the States, we would know. The respect we earned coupled with the Cross name carried a reputation that other alliances didn't dare question, especially if anyone double-crossed the Cross family. No way would Salko return. It would be a death sentence for him and his men.

The sound of dead air came over my phone, which caused me to pull it away from my ear. While I looked at the screen, the seconds continued to tick away. "There is only one reason why you picked up my call without saying a word. Either you're incapacitated, which I highly doubt. Or you are waiting for me to say something. So, I am going with my second hunch."

"I'm listening." His tone suggested that answering my call was nothing more than an inconvenience for him.

"Salko has taken Reyna to Toronto, Ontario, Canada. I need you to be straight with me. Is there any place he might take her other than his country mansion?" I could have mentioned that I knew about Anya Salko, but I thought it best to wait and see if he would be forthcoming.

"If you know about the country home in Toronto, then you know about Anya." Curtis was right, but now wasn't the time to discuss why he withheld that piece of information.

"We can talk about Anya Salko and who she is later. Just tell me if there is any other place Salko would take Reyna besides his home in Toronto."

"Just one."

~9~

Reyna

Calling Kenzi again was a risk, but I had no choice. I couldn't chance the possibility of not getting another opportunity to tell her that Rui planned to take me from the mansion. Kenzi was my only hope to get word to Davian. I dialed her number as soon as Helga left my room, but when he answered the phone, a part of me died. If I had only listened to him about staying at the safe haven, then maybe we would be together. Hearing his voice tore my heart in two. Not only had I betrayed his trust by leaving, but I also put myself in danger and possibly everyone else.

When a knock came at the door, I hurried to hide the phone between the mattresses. I knew I only had a short time to talk before Helga would be back to get me. Only she would knock on my door. If it had been Rui, he wouldn't have been so considerate. And now that she was on the other side of the door, I'd lost my chance to tell Davian what I've denied myself since the day I was taken from him. I was in love with him.

Helga took hold of my hand the minute I opened the door. "Hurry. Mr. Salko will be home soon." Her grasp tightened as she pulled me away from my room toward the stairs.

"Helga, wait. Where are we going?" I asked, coming to a dead stop before we reached the steps.

"I know what is waiting for you when he comes home. I know where he wants to take you, and I can't let him. I just can't." Tears filled her eyes, which were marked with worry. I wasn't sure why, but I trusted her.

Placing my faith solely in her, trusting that she would keep my secret, I headed back to my room. Helga was on my heels. "Mrs. Salko… Reyna. Please, we have to leave."

Ignoring her request, I hurried to the bed and slipped my hand between the two mattresses. Once the phone was in my hand, I snaked the cord to the charger through the headboard leg and unplugged it from the outlet. The dress I was wearing had no pockets, so I tucked the cord inside one cup of my bra and the phone in the other. There was a look of surprise on Helga's face. "Please don't tell Rui. I'm begging you."

Helga clasped her hand over mine. "You can trust me. We need to hurry."

Not wasting another moment, we hurried down the stairs and to the kitchen. I didn't know where Helga was leading me, but she was my only hope in getting away from Rui Salko. When she opened the door to the back patio, the thought of the gate near the pond came to mind. Helga led me past the small table where Rui took his breakfast, and I thought for sure we were on our way towards the mysterious gate, only we weren't. Instead, she led me further away from the house, past the pond and hidden gate, until we reached the end of the garden. If Rui or his men came after us, there would be nowhere for us to run.

Afraid that she might lead me into a trap. I backed away from her. "Helga, why would you bring me here? There is nowhere to go."

"Please, Reyna, don't be afraid." Helga moved the branches from the hedge surrounding the garden. I saw her push open a steel door, similar to the hidden gate. "Come. Follow me."

What is this place? I couldn't go back to the house, so the only option I had was to trust her. I moved closer to the door, but whatever lay ahead was dark, other than a hint of light shining further down the narrow entrance. Everything about this place screamed danger, but I had no choice but to follow her.

It didn't take long for us to get away from the entrance and walk down a tunnel. When we stopped in front of a door, I took hold of Helga's arm. "What is this place?" There was no way I was taking another step unless she told me where we were.

"It is a place I found by chance a long time ago when I first came to live with Mr. Salko. Whenever I wanted to get away, I would come here," she explained as she pushed open the door. "I'm not sure how long it has been here, but I don't think Mr. Salko knows about it. He has never said anything about it, nor has he ever caught me here."

Helga pushed open the door and walked through. I wasn't sure if it would lead to another door until she brought light to the room by flicking a switch on the wall. My eyes focused, and I took in my surroundings. The space wasn't large, and it looked more like a storm shelter. As I looked around, I noticed a twin-sized bed was perched up against the back wall, covered in a colorful quilt that appeared to be handmade. Above the bed was a sheet with a tie-dyed design of pink, yellow, green, and blue, held up by two nails.

I continued to look around the room. I wondered if Helga found this room as it was now or if she added her own personal touch over the years. "Are all these things yours?"

"Yes, other than the bed, which was already here. I have added some personal items and things to survive in the event I needed to stay away for a long time." Helga walked over to a stack of baskets and began pulling items from them. "Whenever I'm needed at the mansion, I make sure to grab food and water."

Helga held out a Ziploc bag of crackers and an unopened bottle of water. When I nodded my head back and forth, she placed the items back in the basket and put it back with the rest. I had a hard time sorting out the thoughts running through my mind. I could understand wanting a place to escape, but I couldn't understand why she would share this place with me. "Helga, why did you bring me here? If Rui finds out that you've helped me, I can only imagine what he will do to you."

"Mrs. Salko…" she began.

"Please, call me, Reyna."

Tipping her head, she said, "Reyna, you have been so nice to me, just like the other Mrs. Salko. I have no one here. Knowing where Mr. Salko would take you… I just couldn't let him do it. I can handle his punishment. I have been doing it for a long time."

"You shouldn't have to. No one deserves what Rui has done to you or me. He is a monster and deserves to die." I would never wish death on anyone, but I hated Rui Salko, and his death wouldn't affect me in the slightest. "When I get away from here, I want you to come with me. You deserve to be free."

"Is that why you have the phone? Is someone coming to take you away from here?" There was a trace of hope in her tone, and all I wanted to do was assure her that someone would come for us. Davian said he knew where I was, but I wasn't sure if he meant the mansion or Toronto, Ontario.

"I'd like to think they will. But I need to know where Rui was planning on taking me. Do you know, Helga? Do you know where it is?"

Closing her eyes, she lowered her head, moving it back and forth. "I don't. When we leave the mansion, they take us in a van with black windows. There is no way to see outside. I only know when we arrive there. It is where we stay until Mr. Salko needs us back at the mansion."

"How many others are there, Helga?" As the words left my mouth, I could feel my stomach begin to churn. I was afraid of what I might find out.

"I don't know. Maybe five or six women. They do not come to the mansion with me."

"What about the other women that work in the mansion? Where do they go?" It was clear she was getting frustrated, but I needed to push her. I needed to know how many others there were like her.

"They go somewhere else." Helga's eyes moved to

the door, and I could tell she was becoming increasingly nervous. "Mrs. Reyna. I need to get back to the mansion. Mr. Salko will notice that I am gone."

The last thing I wanted was for Rui to punish her, but once he found I was no longer in the mansion, he would question her. I knew all too well how he would get the answers he needed. "Helga, if you leave, he will question you about where I am. He will hurt you until he gets the answer."

From the way she looked at me, she already knew what was waiting for her once she reached the mansion. Following behind her, I asked, "Helga, what are you going to tell him?"

When she continued to walk down the tunnel without acknowledging my question, I reached out for her and wrapped my hand around her wrist. "Please, Helga."

She moved her eyes to my hand and used her free hand to unwrap the grasp I had on her. Holding my hand in hers, Helga's head remained lowered. "I will tell him that you left, and I tried to find you, but I was too late. He will search for you outside the gates since I will direct him to do so. There will be no reason for him to search for you here."

"Please be careful, Helga. Rui will stop at nothing to get the truth from you."

Nodding her head, she squeezed my hand and headed toward the hidden door. I couldn't do anything more for her, so I headed back to the room where she found solace. It was only when I reached the room that I felt the sharp edge of the charger against my breast. Pulling the phone from my bra, I switched it on, but it was no use. There was no reception between the thick walls, and my only option was to wait until it got dark before I risked calling Davian. If Helga was able to keep Rui away from the garden, as she said, then I would be safe to contact him.

~10~

Davian

Not only did Curtis give me the whereabouts of this new location, but he used me as a confessional, describing the kinds of things that went on there. Salko was into a lot of illegal shit, and human trafficking was one of them. When Curtis explained to me what happened at the compound, it made my stomach turn. I knew Salko was ruthless with no morals, but to use women and children the way he did made me sick. If I could have, I would have choked Curtis for being a part of Salko's team. But his role in what was done to those women would live inside him forever, and that alone would be his living hell.

It wasn't that Curtis knew where Salko might have Reyna that had my blood boiling, it was the fact that he was already in Canada, and I was still in the fucking air with an hour left before the plane landed.

I needed to focus. My emotions clouded my ability to come up with a plan to be at the mansion and at the compound, five miles away. Curtis couldn't confirm the compound even existed anymore. There was no way I could take the chance that it didn't.

Anger trumped fear as my fist met the hard surface of the conference table while my other hand had a death grip on my cell. I had a choice to make, and if I was wrong, I wouldn't be able to live with myself. This wasn't a decision between acquiring a new company or letting a new investment go. It was life or death. This was about Reyna and making the right choice to save her.

As much as I hated trusting Curtis, he was my only hope in finding her. I needed to come clean and let him know I had been in contact with Reyna. "I've been in contact with Reyna."

"What the fuck? When?" His displeasure towards my admission rang loud and clear.

"About an hour ago. She said Salko planned to take her from the mansion before our conversation dropped off."

"Shit. If Salko is taking her from the mansion, he has to be taking her to the compound or a buyer. I'm going to kill the son-of-a-bitch."

"You're going to have to get in line." After hearing what Curtis said, I wanted nothing more than to see Salko dead, but for now, Reyna was my priority. "Since you are already in Canada, I suggest you go to the mansion. There might be a chance she is still there."

"And the compound?" he replied.

"Give me the location. We will head there as soon as we land."

Before ending the call, Curtis gave me detailed directions to the compound, minutes from Salko's mansion. Leave it to Salko to keep his property close by. Chances were that by the time we landed, Salko would have taken Reyna from his home and to the compound. If Curtis was right about how Salko ran his business, Reyna would remain inside the compound until the transaction was completed, and funds were deposited into his account. Once Reyna was safe, the Canadian authorities would receive a call and Salko's trafficking operation would be shut down.

Patton arranged for two SUVs to meet us once we landed. Nothing was more important to me than getting Reyna to safety. Jeannie and Mathew sensed my tension and agreed to remain on standby in the plane until they heard from us. If everything went as planned, Reyna would be sitting next to me, flying to our next destination: a remote island in the Caymans I purchased as a favor to my father. I never thought the place would be anything other than a vacation getaway.

As we headed away from the airport the GPS informed us the location of the compound was thirty-five miles away. Curtis' text confirmed that he was positioned outside the gates of Salko's home and that he would let us know if there was any movement. I wasn't sure how this was going to end, but we were prepared for the worst. Best case scenario—Reyna would be at the compound, and Salko and his men would be at the house. It was wishful thinking since there was no way in hell Salko would allow his prize possession to be unprotected. Through the years I've learned exactly how he worked. If there was money to be made, he had his grubby hands in it. It didn't matter who he hurt. With Reyna being his next big score, he would have her heavily guarded.

As we approached the compound's location, it revealed a densely wooded area to the naked eye. Heading toward the exact coordinates that Curtis gave us, the compound's entrance was in sight, hidden behind overgrown bushes and shrubs.

Axe was the best trained in these situations, so he took the lead, with Patton, me, and Marcus close behind. As much as we needed Calvin, I thought it was better for him to head to Salko's country home. I didn't trust Curtis enough to let us know if Reyna was still there or if there was any trouble.

Axe slowly pushed open the door while gripping his

gun in front of him. Waiting for any sign of movement, we proceeded down the concrete steps. Once we reached the bottom, we could smell the stench of urine and blood.

"Jesus Christ," Axe bellowed, coughing and hacking between breaths. "It smells like shit."

It did, but the smell of death was also evident. The further we headed inside, the more clearly sounds of moaning and crying could be heard. Anger and rage seeped in my gut and I could only imagine what we would find once we opened the next door. Pushing to his toes, Axe peered through the small glass window and took a moment to look around before settling on his heels.

His right index finger came to his mouth while he held up his other hand using his index finger and middle finger to signal the number two. There were four of us and two of them. Even though they were outnumbered two to one, our best bet would be to create a distraction. Pressing our bodies against the wall, Axe picked up a small rock and threw it against a wall away from the door. Due to the direction the door opened in, the men wouldn't see us when they opened it, which gave us the upper hand.

When the door opened, it was like watching it move in slow motion. I held my breath and watched the door swing open. Axe was on the taller of the two men while Patton took down the other. Rendering them unconscious, Axe zip-tied their hands and legs while Patton and I relieved them of their weapons and headed through the metal door.

I headed into the room first, and the smell was so unbearable that I had to cover my mouth against the crease of my elbow while keeping my 9mm held high. It was dark, but the cages that lined both sides of the room were as clear as day. I could see silhouettes of bodies huddled against the furthest corner away from the locked doors.

There was no way to know if Reyna was in one of the cages, so I called out for her. "Reyna, are you here?"

An almost inaudible whisper came from behind me. "She's safe."

I turned around to find out which cage the voice came from. A small figure sat next to the locked door—her fingers wrapped around the bars. Lowering my body to meet her gaze, I could tell the woman had been beaten. Her left eye was swollen shut and her lip was split, with dried blood from the assault crusted along her chin.

"She's safe," the young woman repeated.

"Do you know Reyna McCall? Can you tell me where she is?"

"Yes, I know Reyna, but not as McCall. She goes by Reyna Salko now." The young woman's eyes filled with fear as she continued. "You must get her away from Mr.

Salko before he gives her to the other man."

The thought had crossed my mind that this woman might have been delusional. But I couldn't take the chance that we were talking about the same Reyna. "What is your name?"

"My name is Helga," she answered hesitantly.

"Helga, can you tell me where Reyna is?" I could see this woman had been through a lot, and I needed her to feel that she could trust me. "I'm Davian, by the way."

Nodding, she looked toward the door before moving her gaze back to me. "There is a place at the end of the garden behind the mansion. It is hidden behind the hedge. It is the only place I knew where Mr. Salko wouldn't find her."

A cry for help could be heard ahead of me. I looked over to Patton, standing near me. "Check the guards for keys."

When Patton returned, I knew he came back empty-handed. I wanted nothing more than to release these women and children, but they were in no imminent danger with the two guards tied up. Reyna, on the other hand, was a different story.

Placing my hand over her fingers still wrapped

around the bars, I smiled and gave her the reassurance she needed. "We are going to come back for all of you. Will you be all right?"

Helga nodded her head. Regret stared back at me, and the guilt soared through my veins as I stood and walked away. I promised them that I would return and, in doing so, meant they would be safe. Before heading out the door, I pulled Marcus and Patton back. "Stay with them until the authorities arrive. I need to know that they will be safe."

"You got it." Patton placed his hand on my shoulder and gave it a friendly squeeze. "Go find Reyna."

"That's my plan." I returned the sentiment by placing my hand on his shoulder and giving him a gentle pat.

Axe and I left of the compound and headed to Salko's mansion. If Reyna was there as Helga said, we would find her. There was no word from Calvin or Giles Curtis, which I hoped was a good indication that Reyna was still safely hidden behind the hedge that Helga had spoken about, and Salko hadn't found her yet.

There was no plan in place on how we were going to enter the property without being seen. Whatever means necessary, one way or another, we would gain access and bring Reyna to safety.

"Davian, did you hear what I said?" Patton asked. Thoughts of Reyna's safety filled my mind, and I hadn't heard one word he said.

"Sorry. What did you say?" I cleared my thoughts and looked over to Patton.

"I know you're concerned about Reyna, but we need to be smart and figure out a way to get her out of there without Salko knowing. You aren't going to like this, but Giles Curtis is our best bet. He knows the grounds better than any of us and is our best chance of finding Reyna." He was right. I hated having Curtis involved more than he was. I didn't trust him, but he was our best bet.

"Call Curtis. Let him know we are on our way to the mansion." I prayed I wasn't making the biggest mistake of my life. One thing that was working with us was the time of day. Soon it would be dark, which would give us an advantage when entering the property.

~11~

Reyna

For three hours, I stared at the walls of the shelter, waiting for Helga to return. I worried Rui didn't believe the story she told him. If I didn't do something, I would go insane. Pushing from the bed, I walked over to the door and pulled it open. According to Helga, no one knew of the shelter, so there was no reason for me to go down the long tunnel.

Pressing my hand against the wall, I contemplated turning on my cell to give me some light since I was walking blindly. The last time I looked, I had fifty percent battery life left. I didn't want to chance losing more power when booting up.

Maybe leaving now was a bad idea. If I waited two more hours, it would be dark. As I turned to head back to the shelter, a sliver of light came through the door leading to the garden. My heart skipped a beat, and I couldn't will my feet to move. Was it Helga who opened the door, or was it someone else?

Move, Reyna.

Slowly, step back.

All I could see was a beam of light bouncing off the walls as I held my breath, utterly afraid that whoever was approaching would hear me breathe. Due to how slowly I was backing away the figure was getting closer to me. I was in trouble, and even if I made it to the shelter, they would catch me.

"There's someone or something in front of us. I can't make it out." I heard the voice say. It wasn't Helga's nor Rui's, but it was a man.

"Reyna, are you there?"

Davian!

"Yes, I'm here," I cried as I pushed from the wall and headed toward the light.

Strong arms wrapped around my body. My legs gave out, and I crumbled inside the warmth of Davian's arms. "You found me." My tears welled. I was finally safe.

"We need to get out of here. Do you think you can walk?" Davian placed a tender kiss on my head before helping me to my feet.

When we reached the door leading to the garden, Axe pulled it open and scanned the area before walking outside. Night had fallen, and the only light to guide us through the garden came from the moon. Before we reached the house, Davian pulled on Axe's arm. "We need to find another way out of here. We can't leave the same way."

It was then that I remembered the gate near the pond. "There is a gate by the pond. I'm not sure where it leads, but it might take us out here." The gate might lead nowhere, but it was worth a try.

In a low voice, Davian said, "Can you take us to it?"

Turning away from the house, I led Davian and Axe back to the bench near the pond. When we reached the fountain, I pointed to the shrubs on the other side of the pond. "It is over there. Behind the tall bushes."

Axe held up his flashlight and walked over to the area I pointed at. Shoving the branches from the bushes out of the way, he searched between the leaves until he found the gate. "Found it. There's a lock on it, but I think I can pry it open."

My nerves were having a heyday. I worried that soon someone would find us and it would be too late. Looking around the garden while Axe continued to work the lock, I was comforted when I saw no one coming. Davian squeezed my hand, giving me an extra dose of reassurance that I needed. "We will be okay, Reyna. We will get away from here."

As I smiled up at Davian, Axe appeared from in between the branches. "Got it. It looks like it leads to a road."

Everything that happened over the past three and a half weeks felt like nothing more than a bad dream. Soon I would be away from this place, far away from Rui and his men. The only thing good about this place was meeting Helga. *Helga!* "Wait! We have to go back." I pulled on Davian's hand, trying desperately to pull him back through the gate.

"Reyna, we can't go back."

"We can't leave her behind. We have to find her." The tears jerked at my heart as I pleaded with Davian to turn around.

"Who, Reyna? Who can't we leave behind?"

"Her name is Helga. She is the one who brought me to the shelter. She saved me from Rui."

"Reyna, look at me." I could only see Davian's masculine lines in the dark as I tried to find his eyes. "Helga is safe. We found her at a compound five miles from here. We really need to go."

It wasn't until after we boarded Davian's plane that I felt safe. When we left Rui's country mansion, Davian found out from the authorities that Rui was nowhere to be found. Their thorough search of the compound and the mansion only turned up three more of his men. In total, five of Rui's men were taken into custody. Three women and six children held captive in the compound were taken to the hospital for evaluation before reuniting with their families. Helga was among them. She was examined and released.

"Why can't she go with us? She has no family. I'm the only friend she has." I couldn't allow her to be alone, so I pleaded for Davian to take her with us to the States. After all, we were going to the same place.

"Reyna, princess. Helga will be safe with Axe. He is going to take her to the warehouse where she will be safe. Kenzi is also being taken there. Rui Salko is still out there, and I can't take the chance that he will try to take you again."

Davian was right. I knew firsthand how dangerous Rui Salko was. He was a monster and would do anything to get what he wanted. I thought about what I went through while under Rui's control. My stomach became unsettled, the bile already making its way to my throat. *Would I ever be able to tell Davian what took place in the mansion? How could I tell him about the marriage license?* Rui maintained it was legal and not a fake. It would kill Davian if he knew Rui and me were married.

Drawing me away from my thoughts, Davian reached across my body and took hold of my seatbelt. "We are about to take off, princess."

Ever since we left Rui's country mansion, the tension had been growing between Davian and me. At first, I thought it was because of the chaos surrounding the need to get me to safety, but even in the SUV, it was like he had put a wall between us. Placing my hand on his as he snapped the seatbelt into place, I met his eyes. "Is everything okay? You haven't said a word since we left Rui's mansion."

"Everything is fine. You're safe." Davian pulled his hand away and placed it on the armrest of his leather chair.

I couldn't let this go. What happened to me was unspeakable, but the way he was acting toward me was much worse. "Davian, if your mood has to do with me leaving The Regency after you told me to stay put, I am so sorry. I didn't have another choice. If I hadn't gone, I would have lost my class enrollment for the next semester."

"You should have told me what was going on with your classes. I could have made other arrangements. You should have trusted me. I should have been there to keep you safe."

I opened my mouth to say something when Jeannie walked toward us. "The captain advised me that we are clear to take off. Is there anything I can get you?"

With everything going on, the last thing I had thought about was food until my stomach roared. "I could use something to eat."

"How about a sandwich and a bowl of soup?" Jeannie smiled as she looked at me and then at Davian.

"I'm good," Davian replied, his tone more abrasive than normal.

Pulling my shoulders back, I smiled back at Jeannie. "That would be wonderful. Thank you, Jeannie. Davian and I can share, should he suddenly become hungry."

Watching Jeannie walk back to the serving station, I waited until she was out of sight. "What is up with you?" I looked over to Davian, weighing in on his crappy mood.

Without warning, he unfastened his seatbelt and stood before me. "I need to know what he did to you. I need to see it for myself. We are going to the back room."

"Please, Davian. Don't do this." I knew what he was

asking, and I couldn't bear his disgust once he saw what Rui had done to me. All I needed was a few more weeks until the bruising wouldn't be as noticeable.

"I saw your friend, Reyna. I saw what that bastard did to her. I need to see for myself if he did the same to you. If he hurt you in any way…" His breath brushed against my face as he positioned his hands on the armrests and balanced his body as he leaned in.

If I refused to go back to the suite, he would know. I was so ashamed of what I had done because I wasn't strong enough to fight back. "If you saw what he did to Helga, then you know what he is capable of." The volume of my voice grew, and so did the tears. "Rui Salko is a monster. I did what I had to do to survive. There wasn't one day that went by that he didn't show his displeasure with me. No man as cruel as him could ever be my father. My mother would never love a man like that."

Davian's expression revealed the hurt and pain my words caused him. My tear-stricken eyes remained on him as he straightened to his six-foot-four frame and took a seat in the chair across from me. "What did you have to do, Reyna?" Forking his hands through his hair, he lifted his head with a deep sigh, refusing to look at me.

When he finally looked at me, the blue of his eyes had turned to ice, and I knew what he was insinuating. "If you are asking if I slept with him… you can go to hell."

The tears that filled my eyes blurred my vision as I struggled to unfasten the seatbelt. I couldn't breathe, nor could I remain seated next to a man who would, for one second, believe I would willingly sleep with someone like Rui Salko. It was bad enough that I kissed him. I would have died a thousand deaths before ever having sex with Rui Salko.

Getting the seatbelt unfastened, I pushed to my feet and made my way past Davian to the back of the plane. Davian's hand wrapped around my wrist, pulling me to a halt. "We learned that Rui Salko wasn't your father while you were held captive. We came across the information during our search for you."

"So, your initial information was wrong. What else did you find in your search?"

The cabin became silent, and I knew he was keeping something from me. Davian was deciding whether or not to tell me. "Tell me what it is, Davian. I'm a big girl."

"Nothing."

"I don't believe you."

"Seems like there is a lot of that going around."

~12~

Davian

There was so much I wanted to tell Reyna, but how? How was I going to tell her that her father and mother were still alive? My heart ripped in two when I saw the look on her face as she made her way to the back of the plane.

When she didn't return, there was so much guilt inside. She didn't deserve what I accused her of. I didn't even know where to begin. I had roughly five hours to figure it out. If it hadn't been for me, Reyna would never have undergone the torture that Salko put her through. As much as I wanted to know just how bad the abuse was, just seeing her told me the torment she went through. She was thinner, and her cheeks and eyes were sunk in. There was no one to blame but myself. Salko might have been the one who administered her abuse, but I was the one who allowed him to take her. *How could Reyna ever forgive me?*

Jeannie appeared with a tray holding a bowl of soup and a sandwich. "I thought you might be hungry."

"Maybe later." I smiled, unfastening my seatbelt.

"Keep it warm. Reyna might be hungry when she wakes up."

Patton was busy in the conference room reviewing the details of our escape to see if there was anything on the security footage that he was able to hack. He wanted to make sure we didn't miss anything that might give us a clue as to where Salko could have fled. Finding Salko wasn't on the top of my list of priorities. I needed to tell Reyna the truth about Giles Curtis.

There was a couple of things that I needed to go over with Patton before we landed. I headed to the conference room, exhausted and mentally drained. I wasn't sure how much help I would be, but helping Patton was much better than thinking about how I failed Reyna. As I entered the conference room, Patton was leaning back in his chair, his hands perched on his head. "That bad?" I closed the door and pulled out a chair across from where he sat.

"Bad is not the word I would have used, but yeah, it's bad." Patton turned my way with a grunt of annoyance. "I got nothing. Salko must have encrypted the camera feed. I don't have the software needed to decode it."

"Well, I guess it is going to have to wait until we get to the villa. You should have everything you need to break the code there. Kian and Darius have been informed of our arrival. They should be able to assist you, as well."

"How is Reyna doing?" Patton asked with concern.

"As well as can be expected." The truth was, I didn't know. I had barely said two words to her about her condition. "She's resting."

"Have you told her about her mom and Giles Curtis?" His question was the reason I came to the conference room. How the hell was I going to tell her that her father worked for Salko and was his right-hand man? After what Salko did to her, how could she ever accept a man as her father who essentially helped Salko obtain women and children to help secure his sick empire?

"Just tell me, how the fuck am I going to tell her that her father worked for the same man who held her captive and abused not only her, but the women and children we rescued from the compound?"

"Sorry, boss." Patton raised his hand in surrender. He didn't deserve being treated the way I felt.

Unworthy.

A complete failure.

Incompetent.

Shoving my fingers through my hair, I looked over to Patton to see his eyes staring back at me. Shaking my head, I rubbed my hands across my face. "You didn't deserve that." My thoughts went into reverse as I remember the reason behind protecting Reyna in the first place. "We are missing something. All this time we thought that Salko was Reyna's father. Clearly that isn't the case. So why would he take her?

Think. Davian. Think.

"I don't know," Patton began. "But let's focus on what we do know. Salko isn't Reyna's father, and Giles Curtis is. We also know that Anya Salko and Louise Braxton are the same person and that she and Rui were married." Patton scratched his head, piecing everything together. "Do you think Salko knows that Reyna is Louise's and Giles's daughter?"

"It's the only thing that makes sense." The thought crossed my mind as well. Reyna spent over three weeks with Salko, and just maybe she could fill in the blanks. "Maybe it's time I tell Reyna everything."

"I don't know much about women, but it is clear how you feel about her and how she feels about you. I think keeping what you know from her is going to be worse than telling her. Just saying." Patton knew more than I gave him credit for. He was right. I had to let her know.

Thirty minutes before we were scheduled to land, Reyna woke up. Her eyes were red and swollen. It was a sure sign that she had cried herself to sleep. Jeannie brought Reyna the sandwich and bowl of soup that I had declined earlier. I was glad she took a seat next to me while she ate. Even though she hadn't said a word, it was a step in the right direction. Once we landed and got to the villa, hopefully with a couple of days of relaxation, I could find a way to tell her the truth about her mom and Curtis.

Jeannie returned minutes later to retrieve the tray of food that Reyna barely touched. Looking back over her shoulder, Jeannie gave us a sympathetic smile. "We will be landing in about ten minutes. Be sure to fasten your seatbelts."

Nodding my head, I retrieved the straps of my seatbelt and fastened them together. As I looked over at Reyna, I could see she was struggling with hers. Reaching across the seat, I took the two ends from her grasp and pushed them together until it snapped close. I thought the rest would make her feel better, but when she turned her head to face me, tears rolled off her cheeks. If we weren't landing soon, I would have taken her from her seat and held her in my arms. Who was I to be the one to comfort her, especially since I was the one who caused her so much pain?

Piss on it. Undoing my seatbelt first, and then hers, I lifted Reyna from her seat and pulled her close before settling in my seat with her on my lap. Jeannie must have had sonic hearing because she appeared from behind the partition. Instead of warning us about the seatbelts, she nodded, giving me a smile before ducking back behind the partition.

Reyna rested her head on my shoulder, with one hand resting on her lap and the other holding on to me. "Am I ever going to be okay?"

The weight of an elephant pressed against my chest—the same one that occupied the room. "We will get through this, princess, together. I promise everything will be okay."

I had to believe that she would. I wanted to believe that together we could put what happened behind us and move on. Be happy. Rui Salko would pay dearly for what he did to Reyna and the many other women and children he held captive.

The sound of the wheels lowering alerted me that soon we would touch ground. Not once did it cross my mind to secure her in her seat. As much as I hated myself for not protecting her, I couldn't let her go. It nearly killed me, not knowing where she was. Now that I had her back, I would never let her out of my sight again.

The Caribbean air enveloped us as we stepped off the plane. The Cayman Islands were like night and day compared to Atlanta, Georgia. The people here had a different way of life. More relaxed came to mind. Hopefully, because I'd also brought Mika here, Reyna would find the same relaxation. Reyna had taken to Mika almost immediately back in Chicago. I thought it would be fitting to have her here when we arrived—a familiar face, so to speak.

Kian, one of the men I hired, leaned against a black Lincoln MKZ as we stepped off the plane. Even though he was part of *The Society,* he remained on the island to ensure that the villa was kept up and secure. It wasn't often that I came here. But when I did, it was only because of problems with the new resort or some other crisis. There were too many bad memories here, but given that my residence here wasn't known, it was the safest place to bring Reyna.

Since there wasn't any luggage to speak of to unload, we were on our way within minutes. I arranged ahead of time to have everything we needed by the time we arrived. The only thing left was to make sure that Reyna remained safe. Of course, there was still the elephant that needed to be taken care of.

~13~

Reyna

A dark-skinned man with a Caribbean accent, who Davian introduced as Kian, pulled in front of what Davian referred to as the villa. Villa was an understatement for the colossal house before me. It was clear that Davian did nothing small when it came to the homes he owned, and just like the Cross Estate in Chicago, this home was spectacular.

I slid from the back seat of the car, already working the buckles of my sandals—more than anything, I wanted to feel the warmth of the basalt tiles beneath my feet. The way Davian looked at me, he must have thought I was nuts. Taking me by the hand, he led me to the front door. "If feeling the warmth of the driveway barefooted puts that kind of smile on your face, I'm sure you are going to love what I am about to show you."

I was smiling from ear to ear. Not because of the warmth, but because I felt safe for the first time in over three weeks. As we headed toward the entrance to the house, the warm breeze brushed against my face. Before Davian could push open the door, Mika was pulling it open on the other side. I turned to Davian, and I realized his concern about my safety went beyond bringing me here. He wanted me to be comfortable, and that included being around people I knew and cared for. If only Kenzi and Helga could be here with me.

As I was suddenly overwhelmed with sadness, Mika wrapped her arms around my waist. "Miss Reyna, I'm so glad you are here. We were so excited to learn that Davi had found you, and you were safe."

I was just about ready to ask her what she meant by 'we' when Lorenzo Cross walked up behind her. I didn't know why I should be surprised. Davian's father was the one who knew, more than anyone, what Rui Salko was capable of.

I had a death grip on Davian's hand, and he could feel it because he turned to Mika and said, "Mika, why don't you show Reyna around while I have a few words with my father before he leaves?"

Mika pulled me away from Davian while he remained outside the door. She waited until Lorenzo stepped outside before closing the door behind him. Squeezing my hand, she led me away from the door. "How about I show you to your room first?"

"That would be wonderful." I met her gaze and

allowed her to lead me away from the entry door.

From what I could see, I already loved Davian's villa. The bright sun shone through the massive windows that graced the home's front. The sun's warmth reflecting off the windows brought comfort. The floor was covered with white tiles, which were intricately placed in a staggered manner to give the illusion of wood planks. I tilted my head upward to a large crystal chandelier hanging from the ceiling that was the large living area's center focal point. The colors brought life to the room. Different hues of all the primary colors on a color wheel were spread throughout the room. It reminded me of a rainbow after a healthy rain. Even the paintings that hung on the walls were dynamic in color.

As we headed up the steps, my hand glided along the shiny surface of the stainless-steel railing. Stopping at the top of the stairs, I walked toward the windows that extended from the first floor to the ceiling, only to find an endless body of water of a clear and a magnificent shade of blue on the other side. I placed my hands on the glass, feeling the warmth of the sun. A smile splashed across my face, anticipating the white sand's texture between my toes and the warmth of the water against my skin. I think of all the places Davian had brought me to, this was by far my favorite.

"It's gorgeous, isn't it?" Mika confessed as she stood beside me, taking in the amazing sight.

"That it is." I couldn't have agreed with her more. "I can't wait to take advantage of the beach and water."

Mika took hold of my hand and pulled me away from the window. "You will have plenty of time to enjoy everything this place has to offer."

We continued down the wide platform that overlooked the main floor until I couldn't see the open space below. Reaching the end of the hall, Mika pushed open a polished white door with a brushed nickel handle. When I stepped inside the room, I swore my eyes popped out of my head. Never had I seen a room more spectacular than this one. "Is this where I will be sleeping?"

"Yes. It is one of the nicest rooms in the villa. Well, other than the master suite."

"This room is amazing." It was beyond perfect. How couldn't it be with a view of the ocean 24/7?

Allowing me to wander around the room, Mika stood by the door while I investigated what the room offered. Just behind the bed, positioned against a half wall covered in marble, was a short hall to the two rooms behind it. As I stepped over to the floor-to-ceiling windows, I noticed it had a sliding door, so I pulled it open. The warm breeze blew against the sheer white curtains as I stepped outside.

Looking behind me, I saw Mika sitting on the bed and watching my every move. "Go on, Miss Reyna. Explore."

I wasn't asking for permission, but felt comfort in knowing that I could. Smiling, I turned to face the ocean, once again taking in the warm breeze. I could have stayed here, just like this, for a lifetime, but I wanted to see what else Davian's villa offered. Just as I was about to step back inside, something shiny caught the corner of my eye. Walking to the balcony, I looked over the edge and saw it was a pool. The water matched the ocean's color, and I wondered what it felt like to swim at night beneath the stars with the ocean as a backdrop. Beside the pool was a line of lounge chairs, which would give a perfect view of the sandy beach when occupied. I could see myself walking over the concrete bridge that crossed the pool just to access the beach and the ocean. But a more amazing sight than that was in the distance, near the edge of the water. Turtles were nesting in the sand. Someone made sure they were taken care of by making sure the water from the ocean didn't wash the nest away. I was sure Davian would know. I made a mental note, it was something I needed to ask him.

I went back to the bedroom through the open glass door to find Davian standing by the door with his shoulder pressed against the door frame. Mika was no longer sitting on the bed. I twisted my body enough to slide the glass door shut while keeping my eyes on Davian. "This room is amazing, Davian."

"I was hoping you would like it. It has the best view of the ocean." Davian pushed from the door frame and began walking toward me. Inches from where I was standing, he took hold of both my hands. "It's been a long journey for you. If you would like, you can take a bath before dinner. My staff has made sure you have everything you need, but if there is something you would like, just let Mika know, and she will get it for you."

I hadn't yet seen the bathroom because my eyes were fixated on the view, but I knew it would more than satisfy my needs. With a nod, I headed toward the two rooms behind the bed. Davian stopped me when he squeezed my hand while placing his other on my cheek. He stroked the pad of his thumb along my cheekbone before he tipped his head and met my lips with his. I wanted to dive into his warmth, but he pulled away. "Take all the time you need. When you're ready, we need to talk."

Talk! There wasn't anything I wanted less as he turned away from me and walked out the door and close it behind him. An unexplainable sense of emptiness pricked my heart. It was then that I feared that what Davian and I shared would be gone. Soon he would know everything that happened at the mansion and I would never get back what we had together.

No amount of lavender and vanilla could soothe the pain growing deep within my heart. Moving the lever to the drain upward, I grabbed the side of the large jetted tub and slowly stepped over the edge onto the plush bath mat. Every movement I made seemed robotic, like an animated movie put in slow motion. The emptiness lingered and played with every emotion I felt three weeks ago. It twisted into feelings of self-doubt and regret.

The bruises covering my body reminded me how much my choice impacted the awkwardness between Davian and me. I couldn't change what happened. But I had to make things between Davian and me the way they were before. *He was worth it. We were worth it.*

Wrapping the towel around my body, I stepped out of the bathroom and into the enormous walk-in closet filled with more clothes than I could wear in a year. Running my hands along the row of expensive clothes, nothing seemed to appeal to the mood I was in. Glancing to the other side of the closet, I noticed a row of jeans hanging below a row of casual tops. Fumbling through the hanging jeans, I finally chose a pair of skinny black jeans. As I pulled them on, it didn't surprise me they were somewhat big. After Rui took me, my appetite became non-existent. As I looked in the full-length mirror, I could see that I was thinner than three weeks ago.

Letting go of the unspeakable memories, I continued to get ready. I found a halter top that looked good with the jeans and quickly pulled it over my head. I was glad that the lacy bra I wore beneath my top made me look amazing, even with my much thinner frame. If only I felt as good as I looked. Slipping on a pair of flat slingbacks, I took one last look in the mirror. "This is as good as it is going to get," I assured myself as I twisted my body to the right and then the left.

As I pulled the door open to the hall, I wondered what the conversation would bring between Davian and me. Before I told him about my time with Rui, I had a few questions of my own I wanted to ask. I wanted to find out what he was hiding. The way he said, "Nothing," meant something. I was sure of it.

~14~

Davian

I forgot how much I loved this place. The last time I was here was the day that I proposed to Gwen. Walking in on Reyna as she was entering the bedroom from the balcony reminded me of the time Gwen and I shared that very room. After Gwen's death, I couldn't bring myself to sleep in that room—to sleep in the bed we once shared. Instead of reliving the memories, I had an addition built where a new master bedroom would be, minus the memories.

While I waited for Reyna, I poured myself a bourbon, hoping it would give me the courage I needed to tell her what needed to be said. Surrounded by everything I had ever wanted—cars, planes, homes, and money, none of that mattered because the one thing I desperately needed, money couldn't buy. I fucked up, and somehow, some way, I needed to make things right. If not for Reyna, for myself.

Downing the rest of my drink, I walked over to the sideboard, about to pour another two fingers, when I heard Reyna enter the living room. The minute I saw her, I couldn't take my eyes off her. I watched her walk over to the windows that stretched the length of two floors. With my drink in hand, I moved to where she was standing.

"I want things between us to be the way they were," she said, and her confession hit home as she took the glass from my hand and brought it to her lips.

"Only you can make that happen, princess, but after what I need to tell you, you might have second thoughts." The reality was, she might never want to see me again after I told her the truth about everything. Her mother. Her father. Gwen. Everything.

Taking the empty glass from her, I took hold of her hand and led her to the long sectional, which under normal circumstances would have brought comfort to me with its rainbow of colored throw pillows and matching throw blankets. Once she settled on the couch, I took my place next to her. Before a word came out of my mouth, I was already regretting what needed to be said.

Taking her hands in mine, I focused on them. There was no easy way to tell her, so I just let it out. "Your mother is alive."

Reyna pulled her hands from mine, bringing my attention to her expression. "What do you mean, my mom is alive? It's not possible."

"I thought the same thing when I found out, but it's true, princess." I gathered my thoughts and rose from the couch, letting go of the only thing that comforted me. "When Salko took you, we used every resource possible to find you. During our search, we found your biological father and, in turn, your mother."

"Wait... my father?"

"Reyna, you have to understand, I didn't know any of this when we first met. I was certain that Rui Salko was your father. It was only through intel we received from your father that we found out the truth."

"Who is he? Who is my father?" Reyna's eyes studied mine as she waited for an answer.

"Giles Braxton Curtis." I had a sour taste on my tongue as I enunciated his name. "The social worker who was assigned to your case years ago was his sister."

As though reality hit, Reyna's shoulders faltered in defeat. "Are you telling me that Mrs. Crabby-pants is actually my aunt?"

"If you are referring to Margaret Curtis, then yes, she would be your aunt." I'd had no idea how Reyna felt about Margaret, but with her name reference, it was clear she disliked her.

The room remained silent for a moment until Reyna spoke, "I think Rui Salko may have bought my mom."

She was right, but I couldn't go there just yet. I had to tell her about her father and how he and Louise met. "Reyna." Her name rolled off my lips with resignation as I moved next to her and took a seat. When her attention focused on me, I continued with the truth. "I know about the things done to your mom, but more importantly, you need to know that your father saved her. Your father worked for Salko. During your father's employment, he fell in love with your mom. Giles Curtis was the one who staged your mom's death. It was the only way he knew to keep her safe. If Rui thought she was dead, there would be no reason for him to look for her."

"Rui knows Giles Curtis. He knows my father is alive. Rui said he took something of his, and that was why he took me. For revenge." Reyna's voice was barely audible when she responded with information that confirmed the very reason I didn't trust Curtis.

I composed myself before saying anything else to her. Maybe telling her about Gwen needed to wait. For now, there was no reason to tell her how I came into her life. If she knew I planned on using her as a pawn to draw Salko out of hiding, she would never forgive me. "Do you know what your father took?"

"No, but it had to be valuable to take me in

exchange."

Placing my hand on Reyna's cheek, I knew the information I shared with her, no matter how she tried to remain strong, affected her emotionally. The tears that settled in her eyes that she was desperately holding back confirmed it. "Reyna, I will never let anything happen to you, but you have to let me protect you."

Nodding her head, the tears she was trying so hard to hold back fell. When she lifted her head, the pain ripped through her as she swallowed hard and bit back her sobs. "There is something else, Davian."

Whatever it was, it tore her apart. She had to know that no matter what, it wouldn't change anything. "Whatever it is, we will get through it."

"Rui Salko and I are married."

My body became numb. Had I heard her correctly? "Did you just say that you and that bastard are married?"

Reyna's confession was the movement of her head up and down. I saw fire, and the calm person I was a few seconds was gone. I picked up the crystal glass from the low table and flung it against the window facing the ocean. Instead of worrying about the mess I caused, I moved toward the sideboard to pour myself another drink. I should have comforted Reyna. By the time I realized my reaction to something that was Salko's doing, she was gone.

Placing the half-filled glass down, I knew I needed to find Reyna more than I needed a drink. She didn't deserve the way I reacted. It seemed like, lately, I was taking out my frustrations through undeserved responses to those closest to me.

Get a grip, Davian.

Chasing after Reyna, I caught up to her before she got to the stairs. I stopped short of where she was standing. "Reyna, wait. You didn't deserve that."

Reyna turned to face me with her eyes filled with tears. "It's not that. I feel like I have no control over my life. My marriage to Rui was fabricated, but I don't know how to prove it. He showed me the marriage certificate."

It was clear the so-called marriage was tormenting Reyna to no end. Salko not only abused her physically, he also mentally abused her. Not in a million years could I understand what she went through, but damn if I wouldn't be with her every step of the way to figure this out, and make it go away. Consumed with emotion, I pulled her close and wrapped my arms around her. "Reyna, you don't need to do anything. Money can buy a lot of things, even the truth. Salko will not get away with this."

Unable to hold Reyna like this for over three weeks

had seemed like years. Drawn to her scent, I pressed my nose to her hair. An uncontrollable need came over me unlike anything I had ever felt. Lifting her from the floor, I moved away from the stairs and walked down the glass corridor that led to the addition I had built five years ago. Reyna nestled her head against my neck, and I could feel her soft breath against my chest.

I held her close as I pushed open the door to the master suite with the toe of my shoe. It was only when I crossed the threshold that I carefully set her down. Kicking the door closed behind me, even in her current state with her mascara running down her face and her eyes red, stricken with grief, she was the most gorgeous woman I had ever seen. "You're so beautiful, princess. I've missed you so much."

"I've missed you too," she softly admitted as her eyes burned deep into mine, almost as if she read my thoughts.

Never could I love a woman as much as I loved her.

~15~

Reyna

I stared at Davian as though I had forgotten how beautiful he was. Every line of his handsome face, I studied, memorizing every feature and the way they came together. How his chiseled jaw under his unshaven face, which was sexy and a great look on him, showed power and confidence that I truly loved. His brilliant blue eyes I loved so much, which undeniably matched the color of the ocean glistening through the floor-to-ceiling windows behind me.

The texture of his hand on my cheek brought me back as he leaned in and placed his mouth over mine. His kiss I would never forget. If I ever lost my memory, his kiss was one I would hold on to.

Davian broke the kiss and bit my lower lip. "God, I've missed this."

I missed it too. Every night I was in Rui's country home, all I could think about was feeling Davian's lips on mine, his arms holding me tight. My lips were back on his as he gently cupped the globes of my ass in his hands and lifted me off the floor. Instinctively, I wrapped my legs around his waist, deepening our kiss even further. No matter how close we were, it would never be close enough.

Davian walked over to the bed, where he gently set me down as our mouths still explored each other. It wasn't long until my feet were on the floor and we were insanely tearing at each other's clothes. I worked the buttons of his shirt while he lowered the zipper of my jeans. My frustration stopped when Davin gripped his shirt and pulled it apart, causing the remaining buttons to hit the floor. The sound of buttons hitting the floor didn't halt our efforts as we continued removing our clothes.

Standing, completely exposed, only then did I realize what caused the distressed expression on his face. "I'll kill him." Davian moved in circles—his hands rolled into tight fists.

As though I was to blame, I crossed my arms over my chest and reached for my clothes. "I should have told you what to expect. I'm sorry, Davian. I'm so sorry."

"Don't you dare blame yourself for this. If anyone is to blame, it's me. I should have never left that day." Davian was at my side before his last word.

Touching a bruise on my abdomen, he lowered his mouth and placed a kiss on the blue-green mark. Twenty bruises along my stomach, back, upper legs, and chest, all in different stages of healing, coated my body. Davian made sure to kiss every one of them before he placed a kiss on my lips. The tenderness that he shared made me feel wanted, but more than that, loved.

Lifting me from the floor, he gently placed me on the bed, where he continued to worship me. He placed his lips at the base of my collarbone, kissing and sucking as he ambled down my body at an excruciating pace. "Davian," I breathed, my body burning from the inside out.

"I want you to tell me what you want, princess." His voice was soft and velvety, igniting my need to be taken even more.

"You, I need you inside me. I need to feel you inside me."

Lifting his shoulders higher, he used his thumb and middle finger and tweaked the tip of my nipple into a hard peak. I was completely lost in his touch as he trailed kiss after kiss down my body. Davian slid one, then two fingers inside before he lowered his head and teased the hard nub of my clit with his tongue.

"Your sweet pussy is a taste I will never get enough of," he said as he continued lapping and sucking while he curved his fingers, stroking me deep and slow.

"Don't stop. Please, don't ever stop," my shallow voice pleaded.

"I will never stop."

Davian pressed the palms of his hands against my inner thighs, willing me to open up for him. His tongue continued doing its magic, pushing me close to the edge of pure pleasure; all the while, his fingers plunged deeper inside me.

Like the fourth of July, my release hit, showering my body with an array of bright colors. Moving up my body, I caught a glimpse of Davian's smile. "Now, it's my turn."

I wrapped my legs around his waist, needing to feel all of him. I wanted to forget everything that happened over the past three and a half weeks, and the only person who could do that for me was Davian. I closed my eyes and shut out everything except what I was feeling at that very moment. Davian did this. He made me feel bliss, comfort, ease, but more than that, happiness. He gave me back everything that was taken. He gave me life.

My nails dug into his skin as if it would allow me to bring him closer as he pushed deeper inside me, filling me.

"Davian," I breathed. Wave after wave of pure ecstasy blanketed my soul, making my body quake and writhe uncontrollably. I felt his back tighten beneath my grip until he gave into his own release.

Lost in total bliss, my eyes popped open, realizing what just happened. Calculating the days since my last period in my head, I began to hyperventilate, worried about what my selfish need would cause.

"Crap."

Pushing from the bed, I hurried to the master bathroom, or what I thought was the door to the bathroom, when I heard Davian's voice behind me. "Is everything okay, princess?"

I turned to face him. "Bathroom."

"Next door," he said, pointing to the other door.

It didn't matter that I was completely naked. The state of my attire, or lack thereof, was the last thing that concerned me. Managing a smile, I walked to the door, reached around the corner, and flipped on the light before closing the door behind me. I pressed my back against the door, taking deep breaths to slow down the rapid beating of my heart. Every breath I took in and out brought me closer to breathing normally. When my mind cleared, I counted back the number of days since my last period. I hadn't had one during the time I was with Rui. Thinking back, it had been at least a month, if not more, since my last period.

My heart raced again. Never had my cycle been so off. I convinced myself that being without my birth control pills was the reason. I couldn't be sure unless I took a pregnancy test or went to a doctor. The only way to accomplish either option was to tell Davian.

My heart skipped a beat when I heard a knock at the door. "Reyna, are you okay?"

No, I wasn't okay. It was what I wanted to say, but instead, I opened the door and lied. "I'm fine, just a little hungry."

Davian pulled me closer, kissing the top of my head. "How about I check on dinner while you get dressed? After we finish eating, we can relax on the back patio."

When I nodded my head in agreement, Davian released me. While I remained in the bathroom, he had slipped on a pair of lounge pants and a t-shirt. As he walked toward the door, my eyes never left him as I noticed how sexy he was. For a brief moment, it took my mind off of the dilemma that faced me. When Davian was out of view, I gathered my clothes and got dressed.

Once I was fully dressed, minus the slingback shoes I held in my hand, I headed back to the living room to find Davian. I still worried about how I was going to tell Davian the truth about my birth control situation, but decided that I only wanted to think about being with him and the future we would share together.

Taking in more of the beauty of Davian's home, I reached the kitchen to find Mika busy preparing a lettuce salad while Davian was standing near the stove taste testing whatever was simmering in a stainless-steel pot. It was a touching scene as I continued to watch them before announcing my arrival. "Something smells amazing."

Davian was the first to greet me by walking toward me with a spoonful of what appeared to be some sort of stew. Holding his other hand, palm up under the spoon, he brought it to my lips. I opened my mouth and allowed him to feed me. When the mixture of ingredients hit my tongue, something sweet yet spicy at the same time hit my tastebuds. It was delicious. "Oh, my God. This is amazing. What is it?"

"It is turtle stew, American style," Mika interjected with a smile.

Just the thought of eating turtle stew didn't sit well with me, especially given the turtles nesting on the beach. "I hope you are kidding, Mika."

"I am. Davian would kill me if I ever made turtle stew. He is an avid supporter of saving turtles. It is conch, which is a sea snail and popular to the Caymanian people."

I sucked in a deep breath, thankful Mika was joking

with me. Looking over to Davian laughing, I wasn't the least bit amused until Mika also laughed. They weren't laughing at the statement, but the look on my face. Soon I was laughing with them, and all the tension from moments ago evaporated.

Davian came around the island that extended the length of the kitchen and walked up to me. Wrapping his arms around my waist, he kissed the top of my head. "I'm sorry. That wasn't very nice."

"It's okay. It's just that I really like turtles.

~16~

Reyna

After dinner, Davian led me through the glass sliding door that opened to the back patio and the beach. We took a seat on the built-in seating that surrounded a gas fire pit, and my sights were on the sun, which was setting in the distance. It was mesmerizing and I could swear I could hear the sun sizzle as it merged with the water until it disappeared, engulfed by the water.

It was only after the sky became dark that I diverted my attention to Davian, and his intense eyes that were staring back at me. Pushing aside a stray hair the warm breeze had caught, I tried to gauge what he was thinking. Could the feelings he had for me match the ones I had for him, but hadn't yet confessed? Was he trying to read my thoughts, seeing the worry that was clearly written in my expression?

Avoiding any further eye contact, I moved closer and nuzzled against his chest with my back to him. Counting the stars above, Davian pulled me closer. "How long are you going to keep inside what's bothering you?"

It was a reasonable question considering my attitude since dinner. I didn't know where to begin or even if I was ready to share what was bothering me. The last thing I wanted was for Davian to worry. If I was pregnant, it would be his responsibility as much as mine. But I didn't want to worry him before I knew for sure if I was. Evading his question, I changed the subject. "Who takes care of the turtles on the beach?"

Kissing the top of my head, he said, "I know what you are doing, princess, but I'll bite. The stretch of the beach on my land is restricted; therefore, only the people under my employment can take care of them. I have a staff of veterinarians and medical professionals who see to their care."

"I think it is amazing. A beautiful miracle. Have you ever seen an egg hatch?"

"I haven't, but I get updates on the progress. Two to three months is a long time to be away from my businesses in the States. There are things that can only be done in person."

I wasn't sure how long we would stay in the Caymans, but it would be nice to remain here long enough for the eggs to hatch. It was ironic that the subject of the hatchlings entered my mind when I could face the possibility of a new addition as well. "Do you think they will hatch while we are here?"

"I will talk with the vet and find out for sure. I can't promise anything, princess, but we will remain here until it is safe to go back to the States."

"Until you find Rui?" I don't know why I asked, since he was the reason we were here in the first place.

"Yes, and any other threats that would endanger you going back."

Soaking in the warm breeze, Mika came through the patio door holding a bottle of wine and two glasses. Setting them on the small table, I debated on whether having wine in my state of uncertainty was a good idea. Looking up at her, I said, "I think I would prefer just a glass of water, if that is okay."

"Of course, Miss Reyna." Mika handed Davian the corkscrew with a smile before leaving us.

I adjusted my position so Davian could move to the edge of the couch to uncork the bottle of wine. My attention focused on Davian until Mika returned to the patio with a glass of water. As I accepted the glass from her, it felt awkward when Davian held up his glass of wine in a toast. "To a beautiful night."

Davian slid back against the couch, pulling me near. I was thankful he didn't question my choice of drink. Come tomorrow, I would talk to Mika and let her know what was going on. I was sure she knew of a market nearby where I could purchase a pregnancy test. I had to find out the truth once and for all.

Davian had most of my things moved into the master bedroom while we were out on the patio. I wanted to protest, not because I didn't want to be with him, but I was afraid of what would happen between us. When I slid under the covers, I rolled on my side so my back was toward his side of the bed. The bed dipped, and I felt the brush of his lips against my neck. As much as I wanted to feel him again, I had to be smart about what this could lead to. "Can you just hold me?"

Davian pulled me close, and guilt hit me when I felt the steely length of his cock pressed against my ass. It wasn't long before I felt the warmth of his breath against my cheek and knew that in the silence, he had fallen asleep. Succumbing to my own exhaustion from the events that had taken place in the last twenty-four hours, I found myself in a deep slumber. Right now, this moment was how it was supposed to be, quiet, peaceful, with no turmoil lurking behind the shadows of the night.

My night of blissful sleep didn't last long. My body jerked with images of Rui. Hearing the scream of panic, I realized it was my screams that filled the room. Terror and fear quickened my breath as I tried to calm myself from the nightmare that took over my body. I turned my head to where Davian was still fast asleep. My body was covered with moisture, which caused my silk nightgown to cling to my skin. I felt like I was on fire, so I grabbed the covers and threw them off before rising to my feet.

Even though my heart felt like it was going to beat right out of my chest, at least I controlled my breathing back to a normal rate. I was over two thousand miles away from the clutches of Rui Salko, but the dream seemed so real. Like he was here in this room, in the bed, instead of Davian. I needed space, somewhere to gather my thoughts, so after splashing water on my face, I made my way to the bedroom door. Giving Davian one more glance, I pulled the door open and quietly left.

After making my way through the corridor, I looked around the moonlit living room and headed out to the patio. Davian's villa was miles away from any other residences, so it didn't surprise me that the patio door was unlocked. Carefully, I pulled it open, keeping my ears open to the sound of any other movements other than my own.

The breeze swept over my body, which caused a brief chill against my wet skin as I stepped onto the patio.

The only light that directed me to the sitting area we had occupied hours ago was the stars and moon reflecting off the water. I felt comfortable here earlier and hoped it would bring me the same comfort again. Stretching my legs across the cushions, I grabbed a light blanket draped over the armrest beneath an accent pillow. I made myself as comfortable as possible by leaning my head against the pillow and covering my body with the blanket. I focused on the stars and the sound of the water as it hit the shore. My eyes got heavier and my thoughts focused on the soothing sound of the water and Davian.

~17~

Davian

I shot to a sitting position in panic when I reached across the bed to find that Reyna was no longer beside me. My mind was still clouded with sleep, but when I got dressed, I realized where I was and remembered the safety protocols I had in place when I bought the villa. No one, not even Rui Salko, could get close to the villa without me knowing.

Moving toward the bedroom door, I swung it open and headed to the main house. The sun had begun to make its appearance, yet the smell of breakfast filled the space as I headed to the kitchen. I was disappointed to find that only Mika was there. There was no need for concern since Reyna couldn't go too far without me knowing. Pouring myself a cup of coffee, I smiled at Mika. "Have you seen Reyna yet this morning?"

It was still early, but of anyone, Mika would be the one to see her. "Yes, Davi. She is resting on the patio. If I had to guess, she has been there for some time. I didn't want to disturb her, so I let her sleep."

Grabbing another cup off the counter, I poured some coffee for Reyna and headed to the patio. There wasn't a day I could remember that the weather wasn't perfect. The sun was shining, and other than a few clouds in the distance, the day couldn't have been more lovely. So perfect that it would be an excellent day to go into the city and show Reyna some of the sights that George Town had to offer. I thought inviting Mika would make the day even more perfect.

Pulling the door open as best I could while juggling two cups of coffee, I looked around the patio until I spotted Reyna stretching her arms over her head. *Had she slept on the patio all night? More importantly, why?* Our eyes met, and a smile spread across her face. "I hope one of those cups is for me."

Taking a seat at the rectangular table in front of where she was lying, I handed her one of the two cups and watched her as she brought it to her lips. Her eyes closed with delight as she continued to sip the hot liquid. Reaching out, I moved a stray hair from her face. "Please tell me you didn't sleep out here all night."

"Is sleeping beneath the stars such a bad thing? It's very humbling. God knew exactly what He was doing when He created this place."

In my opinion, there was nothing more beautiful than the smile that accentuated an already gorgeous face. "I didn't say that, but I may be a little selfish when I say I would rather have you in bed, next to me."

Reyna's expression changed as she lowered her cup of coffee. "I couldn't sleep, and I didn't want to wake you."

Shifting my position from the long table to where she sat, I took her hand and brought it to my lips. Her eyes never left mine, but there was something inside them that made me wish they had. Whatever happened in Toronto was tormenting her. I would never know for sure or come to know the pain that bastard put her through. One thing I did know, I would be here for her, and I would never leave her alone again. Cupping her cheek with my hand, I lowered my lips to hers. I pulled her close, deepening the kiss further. Her body pressed to mine. God, how I missed having her near—the softness of her skin pressed to mine. Sliding my fingers beneath the silky strap of her nightgown, just enough to expose her taut nipple, I made my way down her neck to the valley between her breast, leaving kiss after tender kiss in my wake. Enveloping her areola, I flicked my tongue against the hard bud, enlightened by the sound of her moans against the still morning.

"Do you know how bad I want to fuck you right now?" My cock was hard, and my breath unsteady. "If you say yes, I'll throw away the fact that we are visible to anyone who is watching."

149

"Just touch me, Davian. Don't stop."

The last thing I wanted was to have her exposed because of my own need to take her. Shielding her body with mine, I moved my hand down between us and lifted the hem of her nightgown until I had the access I needed. Rotating my hips, I adjusted my position as I slid my hand beneath the lace of her panties. My lips fell upon hers, capturing her moans of pleasure as I teased her clit with my index finger. Reyna's hand dug into my thick hair, our mouths mating with an uncontrollable need. Her wetness coated my fingers as I worked them between her folds. Dipping one and then another inside, I found her trigger as I curved my fingers to stroke her deep and slow. Her hips bucked upward, and her movements matched the stroke of my fingers in and out of her tight channel. A soft whimper broke as she pulled her lips from mine. "More, Davian. Please."

The sun's light was close to being revealed, and as much as I wanted to remain like this, it was time to give up my piece of heaven. With one last tease, I kissed her gently and whispered, "Come for me, princess."

Reyna buried her head in my shoulder to hide the helpless sound of pleasure. When her breathing finally leveled off, there wasn't a more beautiful sight than to see her fully sated. Pushing to my feet, I held out my hand. "How about we take a trip and experience all that the island has to offer?"

Flinging her body at me to the point of knocking me backward, Reyna wrapped her arms around my shoulders, her lips on mine for a brief kiss. "That would be wonderful."

"Good. How about we eat first? I'm sure Mika would like to go with us." I held her at arm's length, wanting nothing more than to see her beautiful smile.

"You know what I would really like? I would love to talk to Kenzi. I really miss her." Reyna's expression tore me in two. There was no way I could deny her request.

Pulling my cell from my pocket, I pulled up Axe's contact information and pressed send. "Axe, can you please put Kenzi on the phone?"

"No problem," Axe said, the sound of his footsteps in the background.

Gauging Reyna's reaction, her expression did a three-sixty as I handed her the phone. She put it to her ear, and I knew it was my cue to give her some privacy. I pulled open the patio door, but didn't close it behind me. For my own peace of mind, I had to know what was going through that pretty little head of hers.

Staying near the door, I tried to interpret the one-sided conversion I was trespassing on. As I listened to Reyna's side of the conversation, it was clear that she missed Kenzi and was deeply concerned for Helga. If I knew it would be safe, I could bring them both here, but as things stood, it was still too much of a risk with Salko still out there with the ability to track our every move. Even bringing Crosby and Delilah here would be a risk.

Confident that Reyna's conversation with Kenzi wouldn't give me a clue about what was going on with her, I headed to the kitchen to let Mika know of my plans. Even though Mika had been to the villa and visited the attractions of the island many times, I was sure she would be excited to get out. Though she never showed it, the sadness of coming to the villa affected her. Her memories of Gwen were just as real as mine. It would be good for her to get away.

When I got to the kitchen, the mixture of bacon and something decadent filled my senses. I would never forget the first day that Mika came to us. Cooking was always her passion, and through the years, she had become quite the cook. So much so, my father paid for her to go to culinary school, the best one that money could buy.

Catching me stealing a piece of bacon, Mika slapped my hand. "Davi, you need to wait. Your father and Patton still haven't arrived. They should be here any minute."

"Well, they are going to have to entertain themselves, or at least my father will. I told Reyna that I would take her to see the sights and I thought it would be nice if you came along." It completely slipped my mind that Patton and my father would be back today from West Bay, where the newest resort hotel was being built. The Crossbow Resort and Hotel had been a dream of mine ever since my father talked me into purchasing the villa.

"I'm sure Mr. Cross will have plenty to do to keep himself entertained while we are away." Mika was a gem and knew of my father's appreciation for the island and the women who occupied the pools at the Grand Hotel, which was currently the most elite place to stay while visiting the Island, and our stiffest competition.

Speaking of the devil... As he was in the room, he picked up on our conversation. "There is nothing wrong with having an appreciation of beautiful women. You of all people should understand that, son." If my father only knew how much of what he said was true. There was no woman more beautiful than Reyna.

"I won't deny it." I smiled, placing my hand on my father's shoulder, giving it a light squeeze. "How are things going with the new hotel?"

"Things are moving along on schedule. I think we will be ready to open as planned. Just in time for the holiday crowd." My father was always optimistic and usually right.

"That's good to hear," I replied

"What is this about a hotel?" Reyna walked into the kitchen, hearing the end of our conversation.

"The Crossbow," I began. "It is a new hotel my father and I are having built in West Bay."

Handing me my phone, Reyna looked between us. "How exciting. Can we visit it when we go out?"

The reaction displayed on my father's face was not what I expected. Reyna's comment annoyed him. "I think it would be best to wait until it is finished. There are too many safety hazards since it is still under construction."

Even though I didn't think it was a good idea either, it wasn't because the hotel was still under construction. It was more about keeping Reyna safe. Not all the men working at the site had received background checks. It would be stupid to risk Reyna's safety until we cleared every one of them. "Maybe another time, Reyna. We have a lot to see as it is."

Disappointed, Reyna smiled with understanding. Thankfully, the topic dropped when Mika interjected. "Breakfast is ready. Please take your places at the dinner table."

Reyna hardly touched her breakfast. And although I was concerned, I wouldn't bring it up until later when we were alone. After taking separate showers, I shared my concern, but she denied anything was wrong. She was hiding something. Even with dinner last night, she barely touched her food. I thought for sure her spirits would be lifted once she talked to Kenzi. I was mistaken. Reyna appeared to be happier, but her actions said otherwise.

It wasn't long after we showered and changed that we were on our way to the city. Mika finished cleaning up the dishes in record time, worried that we might leave without her. Of course, that would never happen. Not once had I ever gone back on my word.

Since my father had plans for the day, Patton accompanied us. He and I took the front seat of the SUV while Reyna and Mika sat in the back. Inviting Patton was the extra safety precaution I needed to ensure that nothing would happen to Reyna. There was still no word on Salko's whereabouts, and I wasn't about to take any chances.

As Patton drove the SUV away from the house, my cell rang. Looking at the caller, I saw it was Axe. Hopefully, he had some information for me regarding Salko. "Tell me you have some good news for me, Axe."

"If I could, I would. I wanted to let you know that Giles Curtis and Louise Braxton have gone missing. The tracker we had on his phone stopped tracking, so Marcus and I got concerned and searched his last known location. It was just south of Atlanta. When we got there, the only thing we found was his phone. It was in a dumpster in an alley near an apartment complex."

"Did anyone bother to check out the complex?" My gaze narrowed to Patton. His concern matched mine.

"Affirmative. No one has seen anyone that fits their descriptions. My guess, they dumped the phone and headed somewhere they wouldn't be found."

Unaware of my reaction, I forked my hand through my hair, which caused Reyna to address my concern. "Is everything okay, Davian?"

"Do whatever you need to do to locate them. Call me with updates, no matter how small." Curtis and Louise were up to something, but I wasn't sure what.

"Davian, what is going on?" Reyna broke my train of thought.

"Nothing for you to worry about. How about we just enjoy the day?"

~18~

Reyna

The conversation between Davian and Axe had piqued my curiosity. I wasn't sure who they were talking about, but I was confident that whoever it was had Davian concerned. He said it was nothing for me to worry about, but even I knew when someone said "it's nothing to worry about," it usually meant there was a reason for concern.

Mika must have noticed my frustration because she placed her hand over mine and gave it a gentle squeeze. For now, I would let it go, only because I had concerns of my own to figure out. Mika didn't know it yet, but as soon as I could speak to her alone, I would need her help. Once we reached George Town, I was sure that there would be a pharmacy where I could purchase what I needed, or at least Mika could.

Enjoying the ride, I let my mind drift to the scenery. The narrow road Patton drove on provided a magnificent view of the ocean. The white beaches stretched for miles, and while the tall hotels blocked most of it, I still caught a glimpse of the beautiful water. Before I left this beautiful island, I would make a point of dipping my feet in the water. Davian didn't tell me how long we would be here, but I wanted to take advantage of the water whenever possible.

The view of the ocean disappeared the closer we got to the small city. There wasn't much I knew about the small island other than what I learned in my social studies class in high school. I learned that George Town was Cayman Island's capital city, with around twenty-nine thousand people. Davian told me that it was a popular vacation spot because the small island had more beautiful beaches than any other island. I had to agree, even though I hadn't seen too many beaches to compare them to.

Our first stop was Camana Bay. Davian assured me it had the best shopping and I would find everything that I could want. Davian, Mika, and I exited the SUV when Patton pulled up next to the curb near the shopping center. As soon as Patton drove away, we moved toward the shopping center. I wasn't sure what to expect. It surprised me that there wasn't an actual shopping mall like I had pictured in my mind. Instead, canopy after canopy of vendors selling specialty items spread along the street. It reminded me of a farmer's market with everything from sunglasses to candles, to spices and fresh produce for sale. I was sure that most of the vendors were locals based on their accents and form of dress. One thing I knew for sure; the Caymanian people were very colorful and had a welcoming atmosphere around them.

Davian took hold of my hand as we walked to the first covered shop. Mika followed close behind while looking back behind her shoulder every so often. My guess was that she was keeping a watch out for Patton. The shopping center was crowded with people native to the island and tourists. It couldn't have been a more perfect day for shopping. An older woman, about sixty, was sitting behind a table that displayed different sized candles. She was stirring a pot of wax, slowly with a wooden spoon, while adding scented oil to a stone pot with a dropper. The scent of lavender hit my senses as we came closer to the table. I was amazed by how much pride she took in the candles she had created and the one she was about to make. I never saw candle wax being made, and it was interesting to watch her. We continued to watch the older woman until Patton stepped up behind us.

Standing next to Davian, Patton leaned in and whispered something in his ear. Based on the expression displayed on Davian's face, something was going on, and it wasn't good. Concerned, I gave Davian's hand a light tug. "Is everything okay?"

"I'm sorry, princess, but we have to cut our shopping trip short."

"No. Why?" *This can't be happening.* I hadn't had a chance to speak with Mika, and I was afraid I wouldn't get another opportunity to get the test. It had to be today. "Can we please shop a little longer?"

Davian looked over at Patton. "One hour, no longer. Don't let either one of them out of your sight.

I was happy that Davian agreed to allow us to shop a little while longer, but the way he looked at Patton, he wouldn't be sticking around. "Where are you going?"

"I need to get back to the villa. There is something that I need to deal with."

Before I could argue, Davian's lips were on mine, making me forget he was leaving. Maybe this was a good thing. The chance of getting Mika alone would be better. Davian said a few more words to Patton before walking away from the shopping center. The perfect time to let Mika know what I needed from her just arrived.

Pulling her further away from Patton and Davian, I whispered, "I need a favor from you."

When we got back to the villa, I breathed a sigh of relief to find that Davian wasn't inside to greet us. Whatever he had to take care of must have taken him away. I wasn't sure how long he would be away, and therefore, I needed to be quick if I wanted to find out if I was pregnant or not. Mika was more than willing to help me out as long as she was the first person I told about the results. I trusted Mika and was positive she would keep my secret.

Grabbing the shopping bags Patton brought in from the SUV, I hurried up the stairs to my bedroom. Even though Davian moved most of my things to the master bedroom, I still considered this room mine. I felt it to be the safest place to do what I needed to do without getting caught.

I set the bags on the bed, rummaging through them until I found the test Mika had purchased for me while I had distracted Patton at the pharmacy/gift shop. With the small box in my hand, I hurried to the bathroom and locked the door. The last thing I wanted was for Davian to arrive home and find out what I was doing. Filling my lungs with air, I calmed my nerves and carefully read the instructions included with the test. I had one chance to get this right. *Why didn't I tell Mika to buy two tests?*

As I read the instructions, I decided it was best to use the cup method. The entire process would take two minutes. In the end, it would give me either a positive or a negative sign. Removing a small cup from the dispenser sitting on the vanity, I would have the truth in a couple of minutes. Before beginning the test, I weighed the outcome of what would happen if the test came out positive. Of all the thoughts running through my head, the one that caused the most concern was whether I was ready to become a mother. I just turned twenty-one and had my entire life ahead of me. I hadn't even begun to live. If only I had taken more responsibility and not allowed my selfish desires to get in the way, I wouldn't be in this predicament.

Taking a deep breath, I hiked up my dress and pulled my panties down. Whatever came of the test, I had to trust that Davian and I would get through whatever happened together. "Please, God, if You are out there listening, give me more time before becoming a mother."

After filling the cup as best I could, I placed it on the counter next to the white testing wand. Adjusting my clothes, I stood in front of the counter and dipped the end of the wand into the cup for five seconds, just as the instruction said.

Holding my breath as I counted—one one-thousand, two one-thousand, three one-thousand—when I reached five seconds, I let the breath I was holding, pulled the wand from the cup, and placed it on the counter. I didn't have a watch or a cell phone to determine the two-minute mark. So instead of opening the door, I stared at the test wand and just waited. My eyes were glued on the horizontal line that slowly appeared, waiting and praying that a vertical line wouldn't cross over the line.

So many thoughts went through my mind when the two-minute mark passed, if I had to guess, a long time ago. *Had I done the test right?* Could this test fall under the one percent inaccuracy threshold? Picking up the direction, I read through them again when a knock came at the door. I froze, unable to think. I felt like a child getting her hand caught in the cookie jar.

Frantically, I gathered the test and instructions and threw them inside a drawer. "I'll be out in a minute," I replied to the knock as I dumped the contents of the cup in the toilet and flushed it away.

"Miss Reyna, it's Mika."

As I opened the door, the grip around my heart lessened. Mika had a concerned expression on her face as I pulled her by the arm inside the bathroom and relocked the door. Pulling the test from the drawer along with the instructions, I handed them over to her.

I didn't know what to make of her expression as she looked between the test and the instructions. "Miss Reyna, according to this, you aren't pregnant."

"I really thought I was. I did everything according to the instructions and knew the test was ninety-nine percent accurate. Maybe my missed period was because of what I went through and my loss of appetite. Either way, I need to get back on the pill. I just don't know how to do that." I took in a sigh of relief. All I needed was Mika's confirmation that it was negative.

"You need to tell Davi the truth. I see how much he

cares about you. He will understand this. Just be honest with him. He can take you to a good doctor on the island," Mika said, her hand covering mine with understanding.

"Is he back?" I asked.

"Yes," Mika began. "But I don't think now would be a good time to talk with him. We have guests."

"Guests?" I looked at Mika, confused. If it was Lorenzo, I wouldn't exactly call him a guest.

"It's your mother and father."

~19~

Davian

I couldn't even fathom Giles Curtis and Louise Braxton being in George Town. More than that, how the hell did they know where I had taken Reyna? Patton and the rest of *The Society* assured me Reyna would be safe, and our destination wouldn't be disclosed to anyone, no matter what the cost. I should never have underestimated Giles Curtis or the resources available to him.

Losing sight of Curtis was a mistake, but unfortunately for him, once he and Louise landed, my men were there to greet them before they set foot on the ground. So, here I was, entertaining the two people I trusted less than Salko. I hope sending Mika to get Reyna wasn't something I would regret later. I told Reyna that her biological parents were alive, but only because I thought I would have time before introducing her to them.

Reyna had been through so much. The last thing she needed was to be saddled with another hardship once she found out the truth about her father. There was no way I could let that happen. For that reason alone, before I reunited Reyna with her parents, it was my obligation to protect the woman I cared about. I only had a few minutes before Curtis and Louise would arrive.

Pouring myself a drink, I went through the steps of how I wanted this reunion to go. Unlike me, my father felt telling Reyna the truth would be a big mistake. On this, I wasn't sure he was right. I couldn't control what Curtis and Louise would say to Reyna. All I could do was try to steer the conversation away from his employment under Salko and the unspeakable things he did.

I set my disgust for the man aside when I heard a knock at the door to my study. Downing the rest of my drink, there was only one person I wanted to see on the other side of the door, and that was Reyna. When I opened the door, everything, even the circumstance that brought her to me, vanished. My focus was on her and how beautiful she was.

"Is it true?" Her arms crossed at her chest, showcasing her unrestrained personality that I loved so much.

"Come and sit down, and I will answer your question." This conversation deserved my attention, and standing in the doorway was not the place.

I was thankful that Reyna didn't argue and moved

away from the door as I gestured for her to take a seat on the couch. Once she was comfortable, I took a seat across from her. There was a reason for the distance I kept between us. I couldn't allow how I felt about her father to cloud her impression of him. She had to decide for herself whether she wanted him to be a part of her life. It was up to Curtis to tell his daughter the truth about his relationship with the man who kept her captive for over three weeks—abusing and demeaning her in any way he deemed fit.

Telling her what needed to be said, I had to choose my words of explanation wisely, which meant holding back the truth. "Your mother and father are in George Town. How they found us is a concern, but I want to make sure you are ready to face them. I don't want to subject you to more than you can handle."

"What I can handle? Are you kidding me?" Her brows narrowed as her eyes set on me. "With everything I have been through, I am more than capable of meeting my parents, unless there is something you aren't telling me."

There it was. That damned elephant. "I'm just concerned for you, princess." Moving from the chair across from her, I took a seat beside her. "You are a strong woman. Not for once did I ever doubt you wouldn't be able to handle meeting your parents. I just don't want you to get your hopes up."

The reason was lame, but there was nothing else I

could come up with. Hopefully, I wouldn't be the one to tell her the rest. Her father owed her the truth. Taking her in my arms, I felt her breath against my cheek. "Do you think they will like me?"

It was a silly question. She was their daughter. How could they do less than love her? "I have every confidence that they will love you, princess. The same way that I do."

Reyna pulled away from my grasp and focused her eyes on mine. "What did you just say?"

"I said they will love you."

"No, after." Her eyes softened, and I realized what I just unknowingly confessed.

"I said, I love you, princess." It was the truth. From the moment I saw her, I fell in love with her. *How could I ever give her soul to the devil?*

Tears filled her eyes as she wrapped her arms around my shoulders. "I love you too, Davian."

"Then why the tears?" If I could, I would have taken every one of them.

"Because there is something you need to know, and I'm afraid to tell you."

I didn't know what she could possibly tell me that I didn't already know. Loosening my hold on her, I put enough distance between us so I could see her face. "What is it, princess?"

Our conversation was cut short when Mika appeared just inside the doorway, which took my attention away from Reyna. "Excuse me, Davi, but your father, Mr. Curtis, and Ms. Braxton, are waiting for you in the living room."

Mika couldn't have come at a more inopportune time. "Direct them here."

Mika nodded her head with a smile and left the study. Looking at Reyna, I took her hands in mine. "Are you ready?"

With a slight nod, she looked toward the door. "As ready as I'll ever be."

My father was the first to walk through the door, with Curtis and Louise close behind. My eyes were only on Curtis. There was something different about him. It had been nearly three weeks since I had seen him. He was thinner, and his eyes were bloodshot, lacking the cockiness he held when I first met him. He appeared exhausted and extremely nervous.

The placement of Reyna's eyes shifted to her father when I turned my attention to her. Releasing my hands, she slowly moved toward the door where Curtis and her mom were still standing. As I looked between them, the resemblance between the three of them was uncanny. Even though Reyna had her mother's eyes and hair color, there was no doubt that Giles Curtis was her father.

I was insensitive to their reunion, but there were a few things that needed to be said. In particular, to Giles Curtis. Reyna's reunion with her father would need to wait. "Curtis, can I have a word with you outside?"

As though he knew what was about to occur, he stepped past my father and followed me to the sliding doors that led to the back patio. Three sets of eyes were on us as I waited for him to step outside the patio door.

I didn't give him a chance to explain before I ripped into him. "What the fuck are you doing in George Town, and how the fuck did you know we were here?"

Scrapping his hands over his bald head, he looked to the sky for an answer. "I'm in trouble, which means so are Louise and Reyna."

"That still doesn't answer how you found us." When it came to Giles Curtis, I couldn't care less that he was in trouble. My only concern was finding out how he knew we were here.

"Your island getaway isn't exactly a secret, even

though you might think it is. Salko found out about this place five years ago. I don't think you realize just how long he has been watching your every move."

Fuck, fuck, fuck. I wasn't sure if Curtis was lying to save his skin or if I just made the biggest mistake of my life by bringing Reyna here. "You may have just made the stupidest move of your life. If Salko knows of this place and is watching me as you say, then he will also be watching you. Do you realize that you have just put us all in danger?"

"I had no choice." There was regret in his eyes, and even though I didn't trust him, I could see he was being upfront with me.

"Everyone has a choice. It's a matter of making the right one." I was one to talk. More than anyone, I had made my share of bad choices. "Are you going to tell me what the fuck is going on to put Reyna and Louise in danger?"

Curtis hesitated for a moment before taking a seat on one of the lounge chairs facing the pool. "I don't know where to begin."

"The beginning is a good fucking place." Sarcastic or not, I wanted to know everything. I was over these damn surprises.

~20~

Reyna

My mom and I just stared at each other, unable to say a word. My emotions in losing her took over, and before I knew what was happening, my arms wrapped around her, and I pulled her into a tight hug. Nothing felt so right. Even when Crosby and Delilah hugged me for the first time, it was nothing compared to the comfort I felt with my mom.

Holding me away from her body so she could look at me, I was staring back at the eyes that matched my own. "Do you know how long I have waited for this moment?"

"All this time, I thought you were dead. Why didn't you ever come and get me?" A dozen different emotions ran through my head. Anger, sadness, confusion, to name a few.

"Come, let's sit. I will tell you everything." My mom took my hand and led me to the couch, while the man I presumed was my father was still outside talking with Davian.

Before my mom began her explanation, there was one question I needed to know. "Were you married to Rui Salko?"

Tears filled her eyes as she looked up to the ceiling for strength. "Rui Salko is a very powerful man… one you don't want to make angry. He had documentation to show that we were. I guess it was his way to control what happened to me."

"Like he did to me. He said we were married too. He even had a marriage certificate to prove it. When I told him it couldn't be real, he said it was legal." I hated admitting my marriage to her, but given the kind of man Rui Salko was, my mom's marriage to him was no picnic.

"I'm sorry for everything you had to go through. I wish I could have stopped it." Remorse swept over my mom's expression, flooding her eyes with regret.

"I have another question for you," I hesitated, trying to find the right words. "Why did you leave me? Was I such an inconvenience that you felt your only way out was to fake your own death?"

Placing her hand over mine, she squeezed it lightly. She looked past me toward the ocean, like she couldn't deal with my reaction once she spilled the truth. "By now, you probably know that my real name isn't Louise Braxton and is Anya Salko. Years before you were even born, Rui Salko arranged for my transportation to the United States. In order to keep my residency and not get deported back to Russia, he gained documentation to show our marriage. I thought it was because he truly cared for me. I thought wrong. At first, it wasn't so bad being his wife, but then the abuse started. Faking my death was the only way I could get out from under his wrath. Your father…" she paused a moment, diverting her eyes to the patio where my father was now sitting on the lounge chair. "He worked for Rui and witnessed what Rui had done to me. The abuse, the torture, everything. If it hadn't been for your father, I wouldn't have lasted as long as I did with Rui. We created a bond, a trust, and along the way we fell in love. Your father came up with a plan to escape. Rui was away on business, and he left your father in charge. The timing was right, so we flew to the States and made a home. Of course, your father couldn't stay without Rui getting suspicious. Your father continued to work for Rui while still protecting our secret. After three years in hiding, I got pregnant. I tried to let your father know, but there was no way to reach him. One day your father contacted me. By then, you were four. As much as he wanted to be with us, he thought it would be better to stay away. It was too risky to continue seeing each other. Rui was getting close in finding out where I was and what your father did, so we had to put our original plan into place."

"Is that when you changed your name?" I asked,

wanting to confirm what I already knew.

"In a way, yes. At first, I changed my name to Louise Murphy, or rather your father did. Once you were born, I changed it to Louise Braxton. We couldn't officially get married or use your father's name, so we use your father's middle name, Braxton. Giles Braxton Curtis is your father, Reyna. I used your grandmother's middle name and your father's."

Reaching for the locket around my neck, she held it in her hand. "You know your father took that picture of us before we planned my death. The locket was supposed to throw off the authorities. He placed it near the burning car so they would find it. I'm glad you have it."

Placing my hand over hers, emotions filled my eyes with tears. "Why couldn't we be together as a family? You faked your death. Rui assumed you were dead. There would have been no reason for him to come looking for you or for me."

"Because, as much as it killed me to leave you, it would have killed me more if Rui found us and took you away from me. Your aunt, Margaret Curtis, was our lifeline to you. She made sure you remained safe. When you got adopted by the McCalls, your father and I were scared for your safety. We had to make sure you would still be safe. We wanted to stop the adoption. The only way to do that was to come out of hiding. But we were too late. We've been keeping tabs on you since."

"Still, not once did you try to get in touch with me. Why now? Why didn't you just stay away?" I pulled my hand away from my mom's and stood. My fists tightened, angry that she hadn't tried to get in touch with me until now.

"As much as it pained me not to reach out to you, you were happy. Crosby and Delilah McCall seemed like good people. We knew you would be safe with them. Or so we thought. I died when your father told me that Rui had taken you. We had to find you and get you back. It was by chance that Davian found us."

My head was spinning. All I could think about was the time spent in and out of foster homes. There were so many of them. It made perfect sense why I was shuffled around so much. It was to keep me safe. Other than being adopted by the McCalls, there was no interest in me from any family. It had to be because of Margaret Curtis. She never mistreated me, but she was never happy either, hence the "Mrs. Crabby-pants" name that I gave her so many years ago. I wasn't sure if I could look at her during family get-togethers, knowing what I called her.

Worrying about my new-found aunt wasn't as important as finding out if my mom was bought and sold, just like Helga, and how I would have been if it wasn't for Davian finding me. "Did you know about Helga and the things Rui did to her and the other women? Did you know about the place where he held all those women and children?"

Before my mom could answer my question, the sound of the glass door sliding open grabbed both of our attention. Davian's eyes were on me, while my father's were on my mom. The way Davian looked at me matched the way my father looked at my mom. Whatever happened between Davian and him seemed to have followed them inside.

The tension in the room softened when Davian walked over to me and took hold of my hand, giving it a light squeeze. "Your father and mother will be staying here for a while until we can come up with other arrangements."

I should have been happy, but I was afraid that it would only make each of our lives uncomfortable. On the other hand, I could find out more about the seventeen years I lost without them. "I need a break. If you don't mind, I think I am going to lie down before dinner."

"Is everything okay, princess?" Davian's question was directed at me, but his eyes were on my mother.

"I'm fine. I just need to absorb everything. I'm a little overwhelmed." Being overwhelmed was an understatement. So many emotions were running through my head. I didn't know what to feel except confused and exhausted.

Kissing me on the top of the head, Davian whispered, "I'll go with you."

Confusion was pasted on my mother's face, while my father's displayed something much different—possibly concern or, better yet, regret. I could honestly say that I had no guilt over leaving them alone in the study. The weight that was just dumped on me should have clued them on how I would react.

When Davian and I reached the master bedroom, I wasn't sure if I wanted to cry or scream. I wished I could understand why my mom did what she did. Collapsing on the bed, I brought my knees to my chest and took a fetal position. I felt the bed dip, and soon Davin's arms were around me, pulling my body close to his. "I'm sorry that you had to see your mom and dad this way. I was hoping to prepare you better so it wouldn't have been such a blow."

Grabbing his hand and holding it in mine, I clung to him like he was my security blanket. "Why does everything have to be so messed up? First missing my period and now my mom rising from the dead."

Davian pulled his hand from mine away from my grasp and moved off the bed without a word. Rolling over onto my back, I met his piercing eyes. His brows came together in a straight line, and his jaw muscles flexed. I was no stranger to the way he was looking at me. Guilt added to the emotions I was trying to deal with, but nothing could make me feel worse than I already did when he turned and walked to the door.

Swinging the door open with a vengeance, he stopped and, without looking back, said, "I'm not ready to be a fucking dad, Reyna."

Rather than giving me the chance to tell him about the test, he was out the door. I wasn't sure how long I stared at the door when another emotion kicked in, and the tears fell. He had every right to be angry. I was angry at myself for not telling him in the first place that I was without my pills for over three weeks. Wiping away the tears, I pushed from the bed and headed to the bathroom to see if, by some miracle, I could pull myself together. For once, I needed to take control of my life. Davian, my mom, and my father were done playing with my emotions.

~21~

Davian

The minute I closed the door to the master, I could have kicked myself for being such an ass. Reyna didn't deserve the reaction I gave or the words that followed. There was no other woman I wanted to share a child with. The long walk on the beach brought me to that realization. My life would be nothing without her. I barely survived three weeks without her.

It was getting dark, and the tide would soon rise. I walked at least two miles up the beach, and given the position of the sun, I should arrive back at the villa just in time for dinner. I should never have left. Reyna was my world, and it was time I put my big pants on instead of running away every time there was a conflict. It was irresponsible and selfish.

Walking at a faster pace, I hurried up the coast. Figuring out a way to ask for Reyna's forgiveness was the only thing running through my mind as I picked up my pace. When the villa was in sight, I ignored the fact that I was now running.

Bypassing the patio doors that led to the living room, I rounded the pool and headed to the glass doors to the master bedroom where I had left Reyna. My efforts were useless as I pulled the door, only to find it locked. Scanning the room before knocking on the door, I found the room empty. Reyna might have been in the en suite, but something inside told me she wasn't.

Sprinting to the other side of the patio, I swung open the double patio doors leading to the living room. The cold air from the air conditioner hit me, coating my heated skin. The only sound came from the five-bladed fan above me. Something seemed off. I was gone for an hour at most, and the villa was uncharacteristically quiet. Attempting to get some sort of response, I yelled, "Hello. Where is everyone?"

When I was greeted with silence, an uneasy feeling took over. *This can't be happening again.* Pulling my cell from my pants pocket, I dialed Patton and waited for him to answer. "Patton, where the hell is everyone? I'm at the villa, and no one is here."

"We have a situation. Giles and Louise were about to take Reyna off the premises. Kian and Darius stopped them when they got to the gate. We are on our way back now."

"Fuck." I should have learned the first time not to leave Reyna alone. "Don't let Curtis or Louise out of your sight. Whether or not they like it, they are going to be leaving the island as soon as we can make arrangements."

"I don't plan on it. See you in a few."

Patton was fuming. Probably more than I. He trusted Curtis about as much as I did. I wasn't sure how much Louise had to do with this, but I had to believe she was only looking out for Reyna. Nonetheless, this situation could have turned out badly had Patton not been there to stop them from leaving.

As I waited for Patton to bring Reyna back to the villa, Kian and Darius secured Giles and Louise in the guest house. Pacing the length of the living room, something shiny caught my eye on the rug near the sectional couch. At first, I thought it might have been a piece of glass, but when I got closer, I saw it was the heart-shaped locket Reyna always wore around her neck. I found it odd that it was on the floor. There was only one instance I could remember that she hadn't worn it. It was the night I took her out to dinner. The same night I learned about Salko and his sudden arrival in Atlanta.

Picking up the locket from the floor, I held it between my fingers as I worked to get it open. I knew what was beneath the diamond-shaped heart, but for some reason, I felt compelled to look at the small photo. As I stared at Reyna and Louise, the resemblance even then was remarkable. Call it instinct or even curiosity—either way, I pulled the photo out. Something was keeping me from sliding it from the locket. I headed to the kitchen to see what I could use to pry the small photo from the locket. I should have left it alone, but I was on a mission.

After pulling open all the drawers, I finally stumbled upon a pair of tweezers. When I was successful at dislodging the photo from its confines, I found that a small piece of paper, folded in fourths, kept the photo from moving. At first, I thought it was there to hold the picture in place, but as I unfolded the paper, I found a series of numbers written on the back. Whatever these numbers were, they were important enough to hide behind the photo.

Just then, the front door opened, and I could hear Patton and Reyna talking. Quickly I put the photo back in its place, holding it in place with a small piece of a sticky note I had come across in one of the other drawers. Closing the locket until it clicked, I fisted in my hand and stuffed it, along with the written numbers, in my front pocket before Reyna would question me about what I was doing. There was no reason for her to worry about what I found. I'd bet my life she wasn't aware of anything hidden behind the photo, especially since she looked at the picture more times than I could count.

Greeting Patton and Reyna in the entryway, Reyna's arms wrapped around my shoulders. "What the hell happened, Patton?" I asked, holding Reyna in my arms as I looked over to the door where he was standing.

"I'm really not sure. I was in the kitchen, working on some leads, when I happened to gaze out the window to see Giles leading Reyna toward the gate by the arm. I immediately called Kian to stop them." Patton's body language and the rise in his voice showed it upset him.

Releasing my hold on Reyna, I held her at arm's length. "Reyna, do you know why your mom and dad would want to take you away from the villa?"

With a slight nod, she said, "They said I wasn't safe here. My father said Rui knew where I was and would soon come to take me away."

"I would never let that happen." I had to reassure her that she was safe with me and not with her parents, whom she only recently met. "Salko will never hurt you again, princess. I promise."

Remembering that I still had her locket, I reached in my pocket, took hold of her hand, and placed it in her palm. Her eyes fell from mine to her hand, and a smile spread across her face. "You found it. I thought I lost it forever."

"It was on the rug in the living room. Let me help you put it on." My eyes were on her opened hand as I lifted the locket by its chain.

Waiting until she turned around, I lifted the necklace up over her head and waited until she lifted her gorgeous brown hair so I could fasten the clasp at her neck. Her hand was on the diamond locket when she turned to face me. "Thank you for finding it." Something in her words meant more.

Rubbing my hand along her cheek, I remembered she deserved so much more than I left her with an hour ago. "About the other thing. We will work through it together."

Patton was aware of the situation and cleared his throat. "I'm going to check on Giles and Louise. If you need anything, call."

Once Patton left the entryway through the front door, I took Reyna by the hand and led her to the living room, where I could apologize not only for the way I treated her but also for leaving. Taking a seat on the couch, I turned to face her. "I'm sorry for leaving you. I should have never said what I did. It was wrong."

She placed her hand on mine as if to appease my wrongdoing. "You have nothing to apologize for. I probably would have reacted the same way, but I need to tell you something. I have already taken a pregnancy test, and it came back negative."

I should have been relieved, but a sadness washed over me. "What do you mean you took a pregnancy test? When? How? You've been with me since we've been here."

"Mika helped me get it when you left the shopping center. I distracted Patton while she purchased one for me. I got scared. After what happened yesterday with no protection and knowing I was without my birth control pills for over three weeks, I had to know."

"You said you missed your period. How long?" I don't know that it mattered. Even though she said the test was negative, there was still a chance Reyna was pregnant.

"It's been at least four weeks."

Before I worried, the only way to know for sure was to make an appointment and find out for sure. "I think we need to see a doctor to find out for sure. If it turns out that the test was wrong, we will both deal with it. Together."

Reyna's eyes met mine. The way she looked at me made me want to climb inside. So, I did.

~22~

Reyna

The vise that gripped my heart earlier had lessened the minute Davian took me into his arms. He assured me everything would be okay, and that whatever happened, we would get through it together. When he left the master suite hours ago, I knew he was hurt by what I said, but no matter how hurtful his reaction was, he was the man I had fallen in love with. In my heart, he proved he loved me with the words he shared moments ago.

After the wonderful dinner that Davian felt obligated to prepare, we headed to the master bedroom. I should have been exhausted with everything that happened throughout the day, but I wasn't, nor was he. Taking me by the hands, he stood before me with a mischievous grin. "Remove your clothes, princess."

Saying I was nervous was an understatement. It might have been because, for the first time, he was seeing me and how vulnerable I had been. Kicking off my sandals, my eyes never left his as I reached behind my back to lower the zipper on my skirt. My skirt fell to my feet as Davian's sexy grin sent a surge of excitement through my body. I tried to work the buttons on my shirt, but my fingers weren't in sync with the thoughts running through my head.

Relax, Reyna. This is Davian. The man you love. Filling my lungs with air and releasing it, I managed to get them undone. My shirt fell down my arms, pooling on top of the skirt, still sitting at my ankles. Lifting one foot and then the other, I stepped to the side of the pile and waited for further instructions.

I should have felt exposed to Davian, especially since he was still fully dressed, but the way he looked at me made me feel nothing but desired and beautiful. Skimming his thumb across my lower lip, he leaned closer, his lips a breath away when he said, "Beautiful," before capturing my lips with his.

A small whimper escaped against his lips as his hands fell to my lower back and then to my ass cheeks. Grabbing a cheek with each hand, he lifted me from the floor in one swift movement. I wrapped my arms around his neck while my legs found their place around his waist. His masculine scent filled my senses, causing me to pull him even closer. Sinking one knee on the bed, Davian carefully lowered my body to the mattress while keeping me close.

He was still fully dressed, and there no way I could have that, so I glided my hands between our bodies and began freeing the hem of his polo shirt from his pants. Davian stopped my effort, and my gaze met his. "Not just yet, princess. I want your hands above your head."

I loved his dominant side, so instead of refusing, I did as he asked. Raising my arms above my head, I rested them against the soft fabric of the silk comforter. Davian gave me a tender kiss on the lips before pushing from the bed. I knew this wasn't as far as it would go as he walked to the closet and turned on the light. Curiosity kept my eyes on the door as I waited for him to appear. Every ounce of resolve I had was tested only because, more than anything, I wanted to find out what was keeping him in the closet instead of on the bed with me.

I lost my will to stay put and moved to the foot of the bed, then sauntered toward the closet door. When I was halfway between the bed and the closet door, Davian appeared. His eyes met mine with a stern stare. "You need to work on following instructions, princess."

Guilt matched with regret took over. Lowering my eyes to the floor, I said, "I'm sorry. You were taking too long."

When I looked up, his expression suggested I return to the position he left me in moments ago. Rushing to the bed, I laid on my back and placed my arms above my head. Closing my eyes, I felt a dip in the mattress. My breath hitched, and my eyes flung open. Wearing only his pants,

Davian towered above me, holding a black silk scarf. I wasn't focusing on the scarf. It was his masculine form that had my attention. Never would I get enough of him.

Twisting the scarf in his hand, he leaned in closer, his mouth close to mine. "Give me your hands."

There was no reason not to do as he said. I trusted him with my life and knew he would never hurt me. Lifting my arms from the bed, I held them out to him. With little effort, he wrapped the scarf around my wrist. The scarf was soft against my skin, and if I wanted, I could easily remove my wrists from the silky restraint.

Davian took hold of my wrists and moved them above my head. "Hopefully, the restraint will remind you to keep your arms above your head."

If he only knew how hard that would be. I wanted nothing more than to touch his exposed chiseled chest and run my hands up and down the ridges of his hard muscles. But that would be against his request, so instead, I dreamed of how it would feel to touch him.

Davian broke my fantasy when he ran his hand down my neck to the valley between my breast. Squeezing his index finger and his thumb together, he unfastened the front clasp of my bra, exposing my desire for him. A mischievous grin spread across his face. "I love the way you react to my touch. I'm going to enjoy feasting upon every inch of your succulent body.

Holding my breasts' weight in his hand, he let out a moan of approval, causing me to suck in a breath. I was going crazy and needed more of his bridled touch. He was using the control he had over me to his advantage—drawing out the pleasure I was seeking.

Lightly skimming my breast, he reverted to gently kneading, grazing the bud of my nipple, driving me even more crazy. My body was begging for more. What he was doing wasn't enough. "Please, Davian," I pleaded, lifting my back from the bed, coaxing him to take more of me.

Giving me more of what I needed, Davian pinched my nipples between his fingers firmly until they hardened, making me cry out, "Yes, yes."

Lowering his mouth to the taut peak, Davian lapped his tongue around the tip, pushing my willpower even further. Sucking the firm peak, he worked his tongue over it while tweaking the other forcefully. The pain, pleasure, he caused was almost unbearable, but all I wanted was more. Switching his efforts from one nipple to the other, I could feel the wetness building between my legs, and he hadn't even entered me. Rocking my hips upward, I taunted him into giving me what I needed. "More, Davian. I need more."

Raising his head, his breath brushed against my cheek. "You are a naughty girl, princess."

"Only because you make me that way," I said, my body heated with the need to feel him completely. "Please, Davian. Give me what I need."

"And what would that be, princess? I want to hear you say it."

"I need you inside me. I need you to fuck me." I would have said anything just to feel him.

A suggestive grin spread across his face as he lowered his hand down my stomach to the waistband of my lacy panties. With a twist of his finger, he moved it away to give him the access he needed. Rocking my hips upward, Davian dragged his thumb across my clit. My breath hitched with a soft whimper.

I bit my bottom lip, trying to harness the orgasm ready to unleash, but Davian was there to muffle my cry of pleasure by placing his lips over mine in a dominating, yet gentle kiss. As he continued to kiss me, Davian pushed two fingers inside. I could feel my body tense until it adjusted to the invasion. As he slid his fingers carefully between my folds, I found myself rolling my hips along with each thrust of his fingers in and out. Nothing felt as good as this.

Davin curled his finger forward, finding my sweet spot. Moving my hips faster, I was close to coming undone. "Yes, Davian. That's it. Please don't stop."

With each thrust of his fingers, I pulled him deeper as I pushed against him. My body clamped down, and within moments, I came in an uncontrollable heated explosion.

I laid on the bed, completely sated, while Davian pushed to his feet and pulled a condom from his pocket before sliding his pants down his legs. His cock sprung free, and already my arousal was on full alert, ready for another round. *I would never get enough of this man.*

While he positioned himself by kneeling between my legs, my eyes fell to his impressive erection as he rolled on the condom. Raising his gaze to mine, he lowered his body over me. "Tomorrow we are going to go to the island doctor. As much as I love being inside you, I would rather do it with no barriers between us."

I wanted that as much as him, if not more. But for now, having him rooted deep inside me was the only thing on my mind. Of course, the need to touch him was also there, but I continued to obey him by leaving my arms above my head.

Balancing his body above mine with one arm, Davian took hold of his shaft and stroked it a few times before placing it at my entrance. The wetness remaining between my folds allowed him to push inside with ease. I spread my legs further to receive all of him. Movement for movement, I met every thrust with the upward motion of my hips. I could feel him fill me, stretching me to the limit.

Davian reached above my head and locked his fingers with mine. My eyes met his, never once leaving his commanding gaze. "God, you feel so fucking good." His words were raspy as he continued his relentless thrusts. "You will not come until I command you to, princess."

I was already so close to the edge, every minute pushing me closer and closer to falling over. "Please, Davian."

"Come."

His command was like being sent to heaven. My muscles gripped him, and my body shuddered with pure ecstasy. Just like mine, Davian's body tensed, and with one more violent stroke, he unleashed the rage inside him.

~23~

Davian

Reyna was already fast asleep when I returned from the bathroom after depositing the condom in the trash. If it hadn't been for my exhaustion, I would have watched her sleep. She was like a fairytale princess waiting for the prince to wake her. I felt more like an ogre than a prince. Tucking my body close to hers, I pulled the covers over and nuzzled my head on the pillow. There was something to be said about breathing in the scent of a woman, and Reyna had the most comforting scent there was.

The moon illuminated through the floor-to-ceiling panel of glass, and as I gazed across the room, I concentrated on her breathing to ease me to sleep. The thought of Reyna sharing my bed, now and for always, gravitated toward the realization that she was the woman I wanted to spend the rest of my life with.

Pulling her closer, my eyes felt like a ton of bricks, exhaustion finally taking over. My eyes remained closed until I heard Reyna's breathing became more labored. She was dreaming, but the way her body shook told me that her dream wasn't good.

I pushed to a sitting position and placed my hand on her shoulder, trying to wake her from the nightmare she was having. "Reyna, wake up."

"No. Please don't hurt me. I promise never to disobey you."

Reyna's arms were fighting against me. *God, did she think I was Salko?* It was only a dream. I kept telling myself. "Reyna, princess. Please open your eyes." I called out, over and over, pleading for her to wake up.

Wrapping my arms around her, I held her tightly against my chest. Her fight against me decreased, and her body began to relax. Reyna's eyes slowly fluttered open. As she looked around the room, she rubbed her face and realized it was only a bad dream.

I twisted her body to face me and said, "You had a bad dream, princess." I placed my hand on her cheek and looked into her eyes. "Do you remember what it was about?"

A tear slid down her cheek, and when I wiped it away, she twisted from my hold and moved to the edge of the bed. "I don't want to talk about it."

I reached out to pull her back, but she managed to get away. As much as I wanted to go after her, something inside told me to let her go. When the time was right, she would tell me everything about what happened.

It was a sleepless night, and the last person I expected to see in the kitchen was my father. As far as I knew, he was spending the day hashing out details on the new resort with the contractors. Before I acknowledged his presence, I walked over to the coffee pot and poured myself a cup. Reyna's nightmare had caused me a restless sleep. The thought of what took place in Salko's mansion and the measure of torture he put her through consumed my night instead of rest.

Taking a seat next to my father, sitting at the kitchen island, I took a sip of coffee. "I thought you would be tied up with resort matters today."

"It seems like more important matters needed my attention." His remark, although sarcastic, managed to make his point. "What the hell were you thinking, leaving Reyna with that idiot of a father of hers? He's unstable, but more than that, he can't be trusted."

"Don't you think I know that? I fucked up. Believe

me, it won't happen again. I have Kian and Darius keeping an eye on them in the guest house until I can figure out what to do with them." I paused for a moment, remembering the note I found in Reyna's locket. "There's something else…"

I pushed my chair back from the center island and hurried back to the bedroom. My father's voice hit the back of my head with concern. "What's going on?"

Twisting my head, I shot back, "I'll be right back. I need to get something from the bedroom."

When I entered the bedroom, Reyna was still sound asleep. I didn't blame her. The night was filled with her tossing and turning. It was close to dawn before she finally settled.

I watched her for a moment, thoroughly amazed by her beauty. Tearing my eyes away, I bent down and picked my pants from the floor where they were still laying. I reached inside the front pocket and pulled out the note with the numbers written on them.

With one last look over to Reyna, I quietly left the room so I wouldn't wake her. Once I was through the door, I slowly pulled it shut. As I headed back to the kitchen, I glanced down at the note and looked at the numbers. The numbers could have meant anything. There were too many to be phone numbers. Maybe they were account numbers or a code. Whatever the twenty numbers meant, I was certain that Patton could figure it out.

My father was still sitting at the center island when I returned to the kitchen. Pulling out the chair next to him, I handed him the small piece of paper with the numbers on it. "What do you make of these numbers?"

I took a sip of my coffee, which was now lukewarm, and watched my father focus on the note. Rubbing his chin with his fingers, he handed the piece of paper back to me. "I'm not sure. It could be anything. Where did you get this, or do I even want to know?"

"I found it behind the picture in Reyna's locket."

"Maybe you need to ask Reyna what they mean?" My father's suggestion would have been my first option, but Reyna knew nothing about it. If anything, Giles Curtis was the one to ask.

"I'm pretty sure Reyna wasn't aware it was inside her locket. I think Curtis is the person to give us the answers we need, but first, I want to see what Patton can find out."

My father looked skeptical about my decision. "What are you thinking, son?"

"If we can find out what the numbers mean, then I believe we will have the upper hand." It was only an assumption that Curtis knew about the note in the locket, but my gut told me differently. I was pretty sure he placed it there, but I had to be one hundred percent certain that he did. The only way to do that was to find out where the numbers would lead.

Pressing his hands against the granite countertop, my father rose from his chair, giving me a firm squeeze on the shoulder. "Whatever you find out, I trust you will let me know."

"You'll be the first." Every move I made, my father knew, either from me or by using his resources.

Soon Reyna would wake up, and I still needed to speak to Patton. Downing the rest of my cold coffee, I headed out of the main house and to the guest house where he was keeping our guests entertained.

The fresh salt air enveloped me as I walked down the patio to the walkway that led to the guest house. Everything that happened yesterday was a blurred mess. Not only did I learn Reyna could be pregnant, I also had information Curtis shared with me. There was no doubt in my mind that Curtis was a threat to Reyna's safety, especially after he admitted to double-crossing Salko. Either he was really stupid or madly in love with Louise. Given the circumstances, I would have done whatever it took to keep Reyna safe. But taking Salko's diamonds because he got them as a trade for Louise, it would never happen, not by me. Curtis had balls. I'll give him that. So, in his defense, love can make a man do crazy things. Still, it was stupid, and like a target plastered on our foreheads. Curtis might have just put us all in danger of Salko finding us.

With the recent revelations over the last twenty-four hours, it would be suicide for Reyna and me to remain on the island. Damn, if I didn't have to wait until after her appointment with the island doctor, we would be out of here.

Reaching the guest house's front door, I pushed open the door to find Patton, Curtis, and Louise sitting around the dining room table, with Kian serving breakfast. The sight didn't sit well with me since no one should have to cater to them, or at least Curtis.

Meeting Kian's stare, he greeted me with a nod. "I can grab another plate if you're hungry."

"Thanks for the offer, but just coffee for me." What I had to say wouldn't take long since the reason for my visit was to talk to Patton. "Patton, can I have a word with you?"

Sliding his chair back, Patton placed his cloth napkin on the table and followed me outside. The guest house didn't have the amenities necessary to have a private conversation; therefore, it was best to talk outside.

Confusion sat on Patton's face as I pulled the door closed behind us. "Can you tell me what this is about?"

Shoving my hand in my pocket, I pulled out the small piece of paper and handed it over to him. "I need you to find out what these numbers mean."

Patton took a quick look at the note before putting it in his pocket. "Do you have any particular place you want me to start looking?"

"If I knew, I wouldn't be asking you."

"I'll see what I can do. Without a starting point, it might take some time." Even though he didn't look at me, I knew there was something else on his mind. "Is there anything else I need to know?"

I had danced around what I learned from Curtis long enough. Patton had every right to know the kind of danger we might all be in. "Curtis took fifty million dollars in diamonds from Salko. He also informed me that Salko is aware of this property. I have a feeling it won't be long until he comes for us."

Scraping his hands across his bald head, Patton twisted his head toward me. "This just keeps getting shittier by the minute. Do you have an idea where the diamonds are that he took?"

"I think he's lying, but Curtis said someone broke in and stole them from Reyna's childhood home in Gainesville. He was stupid to take them in the first place, but I don't think he is that stupid to keep them in the house where they were hiding out."

"Well, maybe these numbers will tell us something more."

"I hope you're right. In the meantime, I think it would be best to get Reyna off the island. I have something I need to take care of first, but be prepared to leave."

"What are you going to do with Giles and Louise?" Patton had every right to show concern. If I didn't have a conscience and they weren't Reyna's parents, I would say leave them to their own devices.

"Honestly, I would love to see them out of Reyna's life, or at least her father. But she would never forgive me if I threw them to the wolves. I think, for now, keep them here. Let Kian and Darius keep an eye on them."

~24~

Reyna

I couldn't have been more nervous about seeing the doctor. It didn't matter how much Davian reassured me that we would work through it together, no matter what the pregnancy test result showed. His silence during our drive wasn't comforting.

Something was on his mind that he wasn't sharing with me. All I wanted was for our relationship to work. There had to be trust. Angling my body toward him, I looked over, noticing the tension shadowing his handsome features. "Something is bothering you. I can tell."

His hands gripped the steering wheel, turning his knuckles white. "After we finish with the doctor, we are leaving the island."

"Wait... why? I thought this was the safest place for me to be." I didn't understand why we would leave unless it was because of my father. "Is it because of what my father said? Is that why we are leaving? You promised me that

Salko would never take me away again."

"The decision has everything to do with your father, but not because he tried to take you."

"Then, why?"

Pulling the car close to the curb, Davian put the car into park and turned off the engine. "There are some things about your father that you need to know."

"Like what?"

"He double-crossed Salko. Salko knows about my home here. Having your father here puts you in more danger." Davian's eyes softened as he looked at me. "I can't lose you again, princess."

The information Davian shared didn't surprise me. There was something about my father I didn't trust. When he asked me about my mom's locket, he was so angry when I didn't know where it was. I always wore it, but it was no longer around my neck when I went to touch it. There wasn't an ounce of empathy from him when I got upset— thinking I had lost it. His only concern was getting away from the island.

I raised my hand to my neck and wrapped my fingers around the heart-shaped locket. "Before my father tried to take me away from the villa, he asked me about my mom's locket. He was angry that I didn't know where it was. Do you think the locket has something to do with him double-crossing Rui?"

Davian didn't immediately reply, but I could tell the wheels were spinning in his head. Reaching across the console, Davian held the weight of the locket in his hand. "I think anything is possible. Until we can figure out your father's motives for coming here, my only concern is keeping you safe."

Giving my hand a light squeeze, Davian leaned over and kissed me on the lips. "Are you ready?" Somehow, he always made me feel better. The kiss, although quick, was just what I needed to face the doctor.

Davian got out of the car while I unfastened my seatbelt. I pulled the handle to the door as Davian rounded the car. Before I could step out, Davian was there to give me a hand.

Painted a soft salmon color with white planked shutters, the small building Davian pulled in front of didn't offer any indication that it was the office of the doctor who would examine me.

As we stepped inside, a young woman with a colorful headwrap greeted us. "Good afternoon. How can I help you?" she said. Unlike the rest of the natives of the island, she had no recognizable accent.

"We have an appointment with Dr. Ocasio. I believe he is waiting for us." Davian's smile beamed with authority as the young lady began typing on her computer.

While we focused on her, a tall, thin man stepped through a door behind her. He was wearing a white coat that matched his smile when he greeted Davian. "Cross, my dear friend. How the hell are you?"

Davian held out his hand when the tall man was within a few feet of where we stood. "Kosmo, you haven't changed a bit."

I stood back as Davian and the doctor continued to catch up. As I listened to them, I had no doubt about the fondness they had for one another. The relationship they shared eased the nervousness I had with letting a doctor I hadn't known examine me.

Kosmo led us to an examination room where he would administer the test. As we each took a seat, Kosmo removed a white mesh cloth covering a tray sitting on the counter. When he picked up a syringe, my eyes widened with surprise. "Are you going to use that on me?"

"Yes, Ms. McCall. Getting a sample of your blood is the most accurate way to determine if you are pregnant or not."

After cleaning an area inside my arm with an alcohol

pad, I watched Kosmo insert the needle into a protruded vein caused by the rubber tourniquet around my upper arm. Feeling a prick, I watched the blood fill the vial. In a matter of time, he would reveal the result.

When Kosmo left and we were alone, I let out the breath I'd held in. Davian wrapped his arms around me, leaving me with a sense of security that no matter what the test results were, we were in this together. I couldn't help but wonder what it would be.

When he kissed the top of my head, I felt Davian's breath against my skin. "Whatever the results are, we are still leaving to go back to Atlanta."

It seemed like a lifetime ago that I had been in Atlanta. "Will I be able to see my family and Kenzi?" I was so excited to see my best friend and family again that it never occurred to me that I wouldn't.

Just as Davian was about to answer, the door to the examination room swung open. I focused on Kosmo's demeanor, trying to gauge whether the news he was about to share was good or bad. Both of us pushed to the edges of the chairs we were sitting on, anticipating the results. Flipping back and forth between the two pages he was holding, Kosmo looked up. "I'm not sure if this is good news or bad, but you're not pregnant, Ms. McCall. Given that, some other test results have me concerned. We ran some additional tests on your blood sample, which showed some of your serum proteins were rather low. It would explain why your periods have been irregular. In addition to putting you on birth control, I am going to prescribe some vitamins that will help in stabilizing these deficiencies."

While I soaked in the information Kosmo shared, Davian thanked him and accepted the prescriptions he made out. I wasn't sure how I felt. I knew the possibility of me being pregnant was slim, but in a way, it made me sad I wasn't.

Before we left the small clinic, we took advantage of the pharmacy attached to the clinic to fill the prescription. It took no time for the pharmacists to fill the order, and we were on our way back to the villa to gather our things before driving to the airport where the Cross jet was waiting for us.

Despite how I felt about the news, I embraced the thought of not adding a child to the mix of disorder taking over my life. All I wanted was to be back in Atlanta, attending school, and earning my degree. No way was I going to throw away my dream. If I had to do online classes, I would find a college that would accept that kind of instruction.

When we reached Davian's villa, Mika greeted us by running toward the car. She was frantically waving her hands in the air like a madwoman. "Davian," I said as I unfastened my seatbelt. "Something is going on with Mika."

Davian was out of the car before I could open my door, trying to calm Mika. "Mika, calm down. Take a deep breath."

As Mika calmed herself by taking Davian's advice, she could finally tell us what had happened. "It's Reyna's parents. They are both gone."

"What do you mean gone?" Davian asked, holding Mika at arm's length, still trying to calm her.

"Yes, they took the SUV. You will need to ask Patton. He can tell you more than I. He is inside the house. He has a pretty good bump on his head."

Releasing Mika, Davian moved past her and headed to the villa. Taking Mika by the hand, I walked with her toward the house a few steps behind Davian. How could bad things continue to happen?

As we entered the villa, I could hear voices coming from the living room—four male voices, to be exact. Davian was yelling at Kian and Darius while Patton sat on the couch holding an ice pack to his head. "What the hell were the two of you thinking?" Davian's posture stiffened as he glanced between the two men.

"We were blindsided," Kian began. "How were we supposed to know that he and Louise would take off? We weren't out of the room for more than a minute."

"And you guys didn't think to lock the door?" Davian asked, his eyes narrowing on Kian.

"It wasn't their fault, Davian," Patton intervened with a grunt. "There was no way they could have known that Giles and Louise would be smart enough to use the security system as a distraction. If anyone is to blame, it should be me. I should have known something was up. If I had been more alert, he wouldn't have got my gun and used it to get through the gate." Patton placed the ice pack on the table, stood, and walked toward Davian. "They won't be able to get off the island. Their passports and ID's are locked away in the safe."

"That still doesn't comfort me." Looking at Kian and Darius, Davian said, "Find them."

~25~

Davian

The only concern I had was getting Reyna off the island. I still felt Kian and Darius were competent enough to find Reyna's parents, even with everything that happened. I was beginning to think Louise wasn't as innocent as I first assumed. If she cared at all about mending her relationship with Reyna, she would have stayed.

Patton, Mika, Reyna, and I boarded the Cross jet later than I wanted. It was a three-hour flight to Atlanta. We hadn't taken off, and already I was getting impatient. Patton and I headed to the conference room while Reyna and Mika made themselves comfortable in the main cabin. There wasn't time for Patton to research the sets of numbers I had given to him, so we thought two heads were better than one to figure out what they meant.

Once we were off the ground and at an acceptable altitude, Patton and I would be ready to boot up our laptop computers. Nothing about this situation comforted me. Curtis and Louise were MIA, and so was Salko. The only saving grace was that we had these numbers, and Curtis didn't. Finding out from Reyna that he was concerned about Louise's locket only confirmed that he wanted it for one reason, and that was to retrieve the numbers he had hidden behind the photo.

When we finally got the all-clear from Captain Matthews, Patton and I didn't hesitate to boot up our laptops. The best-case scenario was to find out what the numbers meant before we landed. Dividing the sets of numbers, I plugged the first set of numbers into the decoding system while Patton entered the second. There was nothing left to do but to sit and wait while the software did its thing.

I was more than aware that there would be more than one outcome once the coding software completed the analysis, especially after entering a list of potential areas where the numbers could be used. I found it surprising that numbers were used more than I once thought. Everything from bank account numbers and serial numbers to IP and coordinate addresses were used to narrow the search.

Two hours into the flight, the software finally completed its search. As Patton and I stared at the results, Patton thought the results were helpful but still missed something. "I think we are missing the full picture here."

"How so?" I asked, confused as hell by his comment.

"These numbers, -84 01 12 00 23, mean more. If you take away the 23, the rest could be latitude coordinates. The number 23 is baffling since all longitude and latitude coordinates have a north, south, east, or west direction."

He was onto something. Looking at my set of numbers, 34 41 11 99 14, I arrived at the same conclusion. His 23 and my 14 were additional numbers unless it was a code to throw us off. Grabbing my notebook, I jotted down the alphabet and began numbering each letter. It was just a theory, but it was worth a try. Coming up with N for the number 14 and W for 23, I handed my notebook over to Patton. "Look at this. Assuming that you are right, try inputting these numbers and seeing what you come up with using north and west as coordinates."

After Patton plugged in my theory, we knew it wasn't a coincidence that the numbers used as longitude and latitude coordinates would be Suches, Georgia. We were there less than a month ago. The only difference was now we knew what we were looking for. These coordinates meant something, and it was well worth the trip back up the winding road to find out what was so important about this location that Curtis hid it away.

I never thought I would be so happy to be back in

Atlanta. It was home, and the greeting I received when we drove inside the warehouse confirmed it. Marcus, Calvin, and Axe were waiting near the large door to greet us. They looked tired and overworked. Over the past month, I had put a lot on them. Not once did they ever complain. When this shit show was done, they would get a nice little vacation on me.

Before I could assist Reyna, she opened the door and headed toward the stairs where Kenzi was running down. With everything going on, she, more than anyone, deserved some happiness. Drawn to the excitement she and Kenzi shared as they embraced each other, I watched overwhelming emotions and tears of joy consume them equally.

Smiling to myself, I tore my sight from them and focused on the three men standing before me. "It's good to see you guys. Are there any updates on Salko?"

Axe was the first to intervene. "As far as we can tell, he is still somewhere in Canada. Nothing has indicated that he has crossed the border into the States, or flown in, for that matter."

"There is one thing we find suspicious," Marcus added. "There has been more than usual movement in Chicago. Salko is planning something. We got word from Sean this morning. We've contacted Theo to offer him assistance."

"What kind of movement?" I asked, looking toward Marcus for clarification.

"More than normal shipments have been coming in at Chicago's port, and Salko's men have been there to receive them."

"What kind of shipments?" I questioned.

"It's hard to say. It might be drugs, or it could be guns. All we know is there was more than normal activity at the docks." Marcus turned and headed toward the glassed computer area before returning with several sheets of paper in his hand. "Take a look at this. Seven containers were delivered, which is double Salko's normal delivery."

Grabbing the sheet from his hand, I looked over the information. According to the purchase receipts, most of the containers delivered contain dry goods: salt, grains, and sands. There was nothing suspicious, in my opinion. "Am I missing something because I see nothing unusual about these purchase receipts?"

"Look at the last two deliveries." Using his index finger, Marcus pointed at the information on the sheet he wanted me to focus on.

Most of Salko's businesses dealt with importing goods, which, in the end, were to be distributed to factories for manufacturing. The last two containers listed were a reason for concern. The contents were unclassified, with a sub-category under steel and or iron related to automotive materials. This was a red flag. "Why the hell would Salko receive a shipment of automotive material unless there was something else in those containers?"

"That's exactly what I thought, so I did a little digging." Marcus handed me another sheet of paper before he continued with his theory. "I asked Calvin and Theo to watch those two containers. Come to find out, both containers were never opened, at least not while they were there. After the dock hands left for the day, I had them check out the containers. They were empty. So, either they were empty before loaded on the freighter or emptied sometime before the freighter docked.

"Are you sure? Could Sean and Theo have gotten the containers wrong?" I doubted it. No way would they take their eyes off the containers when they left the freighter, but I had to ask.

"Not a chance. The numbers on the containers matched the numbers on the invoice I texted them."

"We need to find out what was in those containers." Handing Marcus the papers I was holding, I focused mainly on him. "Marcus, you take the lead on this. Tomorrow Patton and I will make another trip to Suches."

At that point, everything that needed to be said was

covered. Hopefully, we would have an answer concerning the numbers hidden in the locket. If there were a chance we could leave tonight, we would. But since it was getting late, and given the drive to Suches, it would be too dark to find anything.

When I walked toward the staircase, Reyna and Kenzi had already made it to the upper level's living space. Bringing Reyna here was the best option, but being surrounded by the men of *The Society*, plus two additional women, left me claustrophobic.

Reyna and Kenzi were sitting on the leather sectional facing each other as they spoke. As I watched them carry on, it was clear I made the right decision in bringing Reyna here instead of taking her to the safe haven back at The Regency. Leaving them to catch up, I turned and walked to the kitchen. Even though the kitchen opened up to the living area, there was a glass block wall, eight feet wide, which provided me the ability to watch Reyna while leaving them unaware that I was eavesdropping on them.

Focusing on their conversation, I hadn't noticed that something was cooking inside the oven until Helga appeared and pulled the oven door open. Her smile met my gaze as she removed the dish and set it on top of a woven potholder. "I've prepared dinner. I hope you like meatloaf."

It was hard to believe that less than a week ago, her face was covered in blood and she could barely see out of one eye. There was only a small trace of what Salko had done to her. I was sure her memories, just like Reyna's, would forever haunt her. Just as I was about to answer, Mika stepped up behind me. "Davi loves meatloaf. It is one of his favorite dishes."

I thought Mika would have been put off with another woman in the kitchen, but instead, she stepped past me and opened the cupboard where the plates were located. Shooting me a haughty look, she gave a slight turn of her head.

~26~

Reyna

Taking a sip of my wine, I turned to Davian. There were so many things left up in the air that I needed to ask, and even though friends surrounded me, there was no time like the present. "I'd like to resume my college studies."

When Davian looked at me, his expression showed he was less than happy about my declaration. "I don't think this is the time or the place to discuss this."

In my opinion, it was the perfect time to discuss my future. I wasn't a child who needed his approval to go back to school. "I think this is the perfect time to discuss my future. I am twenty-one, of legal age, and perfectly capable of making my own decisions."

As the words left my mouth, I reminded myself that Rui took me a week before my birthday, and Davian might not remember that I was now twenty-one. I never brought it up to him, not until now.

Moving to where I sat, Davian placed his hand on my cheek and smoothed his finger along my chin. "I'm such an idiot. I promise I will make it up to you."

When he placed his lips on mine, it didn't matter that we weren't alone. My body reacted the way it always did. If it hadn't been for the fact that we weren't alone, I would have allowed him to take our kiss further. Ending our connection, I licked my lips. "It isn't your fault. I will have another birthday."

Pulling us from our intimate thoughts, or at least mine, Helga rounded the glass wall and said, "Dinner is ready."

When we reached the large table set for ten, Davian took a seat at the head of the table. It reminded me of the family gatherings shown on television during the holiday season. With all the excitement of seeing Kenzi and Helga, I didn't realize until now how much I missed my mom and dad and wished they were here as well. Looking over to Davian, I knew it was probably not the time or the place to ask, but I missed them too. "Do you think, after dinner, you could take me to see my mom and dad?"

It was a simple question, but I felt like I was asking for something unattainable the way Davian looked at me. It wasn't like I was asking for the moon or world peace. They were my parents, and I should be able to see them. "I think it has been a long day. How about we discuss this tomorrow?"

It wasn't a 'no,' but it wasn't a 'yes' either, but I let it go for the moment. Once dinner was over and we were alone, I wouldn't stop until he agreed to let me see them.

The conversation was flowing as we ate our dinner. Patton brought up that he and Davian were going to Suches in the morning to follow up on a lead they found during their research. I wasn't sure what that lead was, but it must have been important for them to check it out. When I asked about it, Davian assured me it wasn't anything for me to worry about. Kenzi rolled her eyes in annoyance, like she always did, at the alpha male egos surrounding the table. God, I missed her.

I don't know what came over me, but I gave Kenzi a mischievous look and let my inner diva come out. "I would like to make the trip with you and Patton."

One thing was certain. I got their attention when Patton and Davian said, "No," in unison.

"There is no reason for you to go with us. It will be a short trip, there and back." Davian said, his hand fell to mine with a soft squeeze. "Besides, I think Kenzi would like to spend more time catching up with you. You two could work out the details of your classes."

"Are you saying what I think you are?" My stomach

was doing somersaults, knowing that I would back in college.

"I've given it some thought. I don't see any reason you can't take an online class at GSU." Davian gave me a wink and a sincere smile.

I could have jumped across the table and given Davian a big kiss. Since we arrived back in Atlanta, bringing up the subject of going back to school had been like a bad toothache. But, now, the painful thought of never returning to school was gone. I owed Davian my life. He saved me. I finally understood how important it was for him to keep me safe. Having spent time with Rui Salko, I'd be stupid not to listen to him. Taking online classes was better than not going to classes at all.

Dinner ended on a great note. The guys headed back down the stairs while Kenzi, Mika, and I helped Helga with the dishes. I said nothing more about my parents, but that didn't mean I wouldn't bring it up again once Davian and I were alone. I was buzzing with excitement and wanted to get the dishes done so Kenzi and I could begin looking at the GSU website to find out what was necessary to take the online classes I needed to graduate. I was behind on my studies, and with everything that happened, I needed to work extra hard to get caught up. Kenzi decided when I disappeared to take the semester away from school. Now that I was back, there was no reason for her not to go back. I couldn't imagine how hard it was for her. I was sure she was going crazy with worry.

Once the dishes were cleaned and put away, we relaxed in the living room. The guys were still downstairs doing whatever they did. It was nice hanging out with the girls, which I hadn't done in a long time.

Doing what girls do, which is mostly gossip. Kenzi surprised me when she blurted out, "I think we should have a party for you."

With her eyes directed at me, it was obvious I was the "you" she was referring to. "A party. What kind of party?"

"For your birthday. You turned twenty-one over two weeks ago and deserve to have a party."

"I think that is a great idea," Helga said, adjusting her position on the couch so she could see all of our faces.

"Me too." Mika proudly stood, her hands coming to her chest.

"I think all of you are nuts. Besides, Davian would never go for a party. My safety is his top concern." I looked between them, and we all giggled together as I tried to impersonate his manly voice on the last statement.

The room grew silent after all the laughter stopped.

The realization of having a party was out of reach until Mika said, "Let me talk to Davi. I can change his mind. He loves you, Reyna, and I'm pretty sure he would do anything for you."

After Mika showed me to Davian's bedroom, I couldn't help but wonder if Helga, Mika, and Kenzi could pull off a twenty-first birthday party for me. I wasn't even sure if Davian would agree. Ever since Rui took me, he had been extra careful about keeping me safe. Having a party would be good for everyone's morale. It might even ease some of the tension we'd all felt the past couple of weeks. These women were like sisters, and the last thing I wanted was for them to be disappointed. Hopefully, after Mika talked with Davian, he would agree.

Mentally exhausted, I pulled my silk nightgown from my suitcase and began undressing. I wasn't sure how late Davian would be downstairs working, but I wanted to stay awake to talk to him. Mostly, I wanted to know when I could see my mom and dad.

The buzz from the wine I drank was wearing off, and I could barely keep my eyes open. Gathering the robe I placed over the armchair next to the dresser, I quickly put it on and headed out of the room. The living area was quiet, which told me I was the only one awake other than the guys who were still downstairs working away. As I padded down the stairs in my bare feet, I could hear two male voices in what appeared to be a heated conversation.

It was hard to tell who was arguing since the smoky glass hid the computer area. Of the men arguing, neither one of them was Davian. Of that, I was sure. When I reached the bottom of the stairs and rounded the glass-enclosed room, I was met with Davian's steely eyes. A grin appeared across his face as his eyes moved down the length of my body. My robe fell open, revealing my nightgown, which was less than appropriate for any eyes other than his.

Pulling the two sides of the robe together to cover my nightgown that came to mid-thigh, I tied the sash. "I heard some arguing. Is everything okay?"

"The guys have a habit of showing each other who is more knowledgeable. It's nothing. I'm exhausted," he replied, reaching for my hand before leading me back up the stairs. "Let's go to bed."

I wasn't sure if what Davian had said was entirely accurate, but I didn't pursue finding out why they were arguing. There was something more important weighing on my mind. "Have you thought more about letting me see my parents?"

Unbuttoning his shirt as he kicked off his shoes, his

eyes studied me. "I have. I've contacted them, and they will be here in the morning."

As powerful and dominant as Davian was, he never ceased to amaze me. I never knew from one minute to the next what he would say or do. Wrapping my arms around his broad shoulders, I placed my lips on his. "Thank you for understanding."

The same grin I saw moments ago returned. Lifting me from the floor, I wrapped my legs around his waist as he walked me over to the bed. Heat and desire flooded my body, consuming me with the need to feel him deep inside me. It wasn't the wine that had my head spinning. It was the unequivocal craving that only he could satisfy.

"I thought you were exhausted," I said. Davian's need was parallel to mine, even with his exhaustion.

"I'm never too tired to take what is mine."

His dominant confession made me wetter than I already was. I loved the way he claimed my body as his. "Then, take me as you wish." It was a bold statement, but I was aware from the beginning that he was holding back his true desires.

"Be careful, princess. You have no idea what you are offering."

"I'm yours, Davian. I want to share everything with you." It was true. I loved him, and with that came trust.

Pushing from the bed, Davian lowered his pants and boxers while removing the condom he always conveniently tucked away in his wallet. Setting it on the nightstand, I kept my eyes on him as he walked to the closet on the other side of the large room. I would never get tired of his body. His broad shoulders, his sculpted abs—mostly the strength and warmth of his arms as he held me tight.

Davian returned to the bed holding several items. A scarf, handcuffs, and something I didn't recognize, nor knew what it was used for. Placing the items on the bed, he straddled my body. "I want you to give me your body, Princess. I want you to trust me completely."

Nodding my head, I trusted him completely. Heart. Body. And soul.

"I need you to say it, Reyna."

"I trust you, Davian. I trust you with my body. Completely."

Kneeling between my legs, Davian pushed up the hem of my nightgown, revealing the lace thong that matched the nightgown. I moved to a sitting position, allowing Davian to lift the gown up and over my head. Smiling, there was only desire in his eyes. "Beautiful."

My body heated at his declaration, and there was no doubt he would find my thong soaked when he removed it. Placing a kiss on my lips, which set me on fire, he moved lower down my body. Davian's breath left me undone, sensitizing my skin with need. Thrusting my hips upward, I wanted him to take me before I exploded. "Please, Davian."

"Patience, princess."

Patience was the last thing I had, and my desire to be taken doubled as he picked up the scarf he placed on the bed and secured it behind my head, blocking my vision. Anticipating what was to come next, my senses were heightened when I felt the handcuffs' cold metal around my wrists as he positioned them above my head. I should have been concerned, but I trusted Davian. Whatever he had planned, it would be unforgettable.

Without warning, he lowered his mouth to my belly, my thighs, making sure he kissed every inch of my exposed skin. The sound of foil being torn pierced my ears. Inserting one finger and then another into my channel, Davian brought his mouth to mine, treating me to a soft kiss. "Do you know how perfect you are?"

"Show me."

I felt Davian adjust his position. Taking hold of my hips, he lifted my legs from the bed and wrapped them around his waist. He lingered there with no movement, and even though I couldn't see him, I knew he was taking great pleasure from the torment he was putting me through. Lifting my cuffed hands from above my head, I lowered them down my body. I reached between my legs, my fingers close to finding the spot that desperately needed some tender loving care. If he wasn't going to take care of me, I would.

"Hands above your head, princess. This is mine to worship." Davian's voice was commanding as the palm of his hand met my ass, leaving a slight sting.

Moving my hands above my head, I obeyed him with reservations. "I need to come, Davian."

Pinning my hands above my head, Davian brought his mouth to my ear. "Be a good girl, and let me take what is mine."

Before I could protest, he entered me with strong, even strokes, giving me what I needed. Gripping my hips, he angled his body to thrust even deeper. In one final powerful thrust, he hit home, taking my release with him.

I was his.

Totally.

Completely.

~27~

Davian

While I dressed, my eyes fell upon Reyna as she laid on the bed like an angel. My lust for her rose as I remembered last night and the way her perfect tits bounced with each thrust inside her. The thought of losing her sent an ache to my heart, which made me thankful that I had her back. Morning sex would have been amazing, but Patton was waiting, and I wanted to get an early start to Suches so we would be back before nightfall. I promised Reyna I would never leave her, but she was in good hands. Other than the safe haven back at The Regency, the warehouse was the safest place for her to be.

Closing the door behind me, I headed to the kitchen to grab a cup of coffee before heading downstairs. Mika was already awake, which didn't surprise me. The smell of breakfast blanketed the kitchen, and soon everyone would be awake.

Flipping over one of the cups she had laid out on the counter, I filled it to the rim. Taking a sip, I snatched one of her signature muffins while her back was towards me. "You never could resist my blueberry muffins."

It was a fact. Mika's muffins were the best in Georgia. "Do you blame me?"

Turning to face me, she placed her hands on the counter. "Can I ask you something?"

"You know you can ask me anything, Mika." Mika never asked for permission to say what was on her mind. I never wanted her to think that she couldn't.

"I think it would be a wonderful idea to have a twenty-first birthday party for Reyna. The other women and I have been talking. Reyna never had one, and it would be nice. After all, she is only twenty-one once."

Taking another sip, I leaned in like I was letting her in on a secret. "I think that is a wonderful idea. I was just thinking about doing something for her myself." It had been only a passing idea arising from a conversation Reyna and I had yesterday, but I couldn't let Mika know it hadn't been on my mind.

"I'm glad you agree. I'll let you know what we come up with. I think Mr. and Mrs. McCall should be here when we celebrate her birthday," Mika said, rearranging the muffins on the platter so it didn't look like I had taken one.

"Let me know what you need me to do." Only having attended parties, I had no clue what went into planning a twenty-first birthday. Whenever I had an event to plan, Samantha, my general manager, always took care of the details.

As I made my way down the stairs, Patton was on his way up. Stopping with two steps between us, he looked up. "The SUV is fueled. I'm ready to go whenever you are."

"Let's go so we can get back before dark," I replied, as I waited for him to turn before I followed him down the stairs.

After loading the SUV with tools we thought we would need, Patton pulled away from the warehouse. Looking back at the garage door closing through the side mirror, I couldn't stop thinking about what we would find once we reached Suches. Curtis admitted he stole fifty million dollars in diamonds from Salko as payment for what he did to Louise. I couldn't help but wonder if the diamonds would be what we would find. It wasn't impossible to think, mostly because of his concern for Reyna's locket.

Once we were close to Suches, I plugged the coordinates into the reverse Geo-tracker and waited for the location to show up on the screen. Unlike what I had expected, the location was inside the city limits of Suches and not along Suches Loop. It was totally unexpected since Louise's so-called accident happened there.

"Are you seeing this?" I turned to Patton to see his reaction.

Patton dropped his gaze to the tracker. "Are you sure you put in the right coordinates?"

Looking down at the coordinates I had written down, I double-checked them against the ones I had entered. "They are spot on. I guess we will have to see what we find there. Maybe there is a reason Curtis chose this spot."

Twenty minutes later, Patton pulled up to a residence just north of Woody Lake. The property appeared deserted. Patton stopped the SUV and turned off the engine. As I looked around, the property was definitely abandoned. It reminded me of a scene from the movie *Deliverance*. Three rusted truck frames occupied the northeast corner of the property, hidden by weeds about three feet high. On the other side of the property was an old shed that looked like it could collapse at any minute. "What is this place?" I looked over to Patton as he held the Geo-tracker in his hand.

"I don't know, but let's find these coordinates so we can get out of here."

"I couldn't agree more."

Once we exited the SUV, I followed Patton near a wooded area behind the shed. He paused for a moment, looking between the trees that overtook the grounds. "I think we better grab a shovel. If what we are looking for is somewhere in this wooded area, I have a feeling we are going to need it."

Jogging back to the SUV, I popped the liftgate and grabbed two shovels. Holding one in each hand, I hurried back to Patton waiting on the edge of the tree line. I handed him a shovel and we made our way through the trees. The signal on the tracker started to beep, which told us we were close. The more frequent the beep, the closer we were. At one point during our search, the beeping stopped. It was an indication that we were going in the wrong direction, according to Patton. Switching our direction, the beeping once again resumed.

We continued to move deeper into the wooded area; the tracker took us further away from where we parked. The trees were so thick that only a sliver of light could be seen. It was only when the tracker gave off a steady beep that we knew we had reached the coordinates we were tracking. We were in the middle of nowhere, at least a mile away from where we parked. There was no reason to believe this was a setup. No one knew we were here. The numbers meant something. We had to take a risk, so without hesitation, we began digging away the leaf-covered soil.

The pile of dirt, about three feet high, continued to grow until the tip of Patton's shovel hit something. "I think we're here."

Kneeling, we began to use our hands to push away the remaining dirt. Hidden beneath the ground was a black duffle bag wrapped in thick black plastic. My only thought was at least Curtis was smart enough to think about the elements and the bag's survival. We pulled away the plastic secured around the bag with duct tape until the only thing that remained was the bag. We were surprised it was in good condition after being buried for as long as it was.

Patton pulled the zipper back, revealing several black velvet cases inside. Taking one in his hand, he pulled it open. It was no surprise to me that the box was filled with diamonds. The same diamonds that Curtis had stolen from Salko.

"Wow! I wasn't expecting to find these." Patton's face matched his reaction as he picked up a handful of the small diamonds and held it out in his hand. "Do you think these are real?"

I told him about Curtis's confession, but it was still unbelievable that we found them. "They're real. When Curtis told me he had stolen them from Salko years ago, I guess I never thought that we would actually find them."

Patton put the diamonds back in the velvet box and snapped the lid shut. "What now?"

"I have a plan." I knew exactly what I was going to do, and it didn't include giving the diamonds back to Salko or Curtis. As dangerous as it was keeping fifty million dollars in diamonds, it would give me the power I needed to bring Salko down once and for all.

After carefully filling the hole with the dirt so the ground looked undisturbed, we walked back to the SUV with the black bag. I was already thinking of how I could use the diamonds against Salko and Curtis. As far as Salko knew, Curtis still had the diamonds in his possession. There was no reason for him to think otherwise. It was safe to speculate that Curtis needed the coordinates to find where he buried the diamonds. Otherwise, he would have already dug them up. Without the exact coordinates, he would be digging holes for a very long time.

When we arrived at the warehouse, I could see through the computer room entrance. The guys were congregated around Calvin, looking at something on his computer screen. Instead of finding out what had their attention, I headed up the stairs with the black bag filled with diamonds. When I reached the top of the stairs, I was glad that I didn't have to explain what was inside. The living area was unoccupied, and so was the kitchen. I almost hightailed it back downstairs when I heard laughter coming from one of the bedrooms.

With a smile, I headed toward the two secured rooms where we kept the weapons. Inside the other room was a fireproof safe that required my fingerprint to open. I wasn't like I didn't trust the men. I just didn't want them put in a situation where someone could hold it against them.

Knowing the diamonds were secured in the safe, my focus shifted to what was so interesting on Calvin's computer. Even though I could no longer hear laughter as I headed down the stairs, the light was still on in the bedroom, letting me know the girls were still together. Something inside, probably my intuition, told me to check on them before heading downstairs.

Turning on my heels, I made my way to the bedroom closest to the kitchen. When I tapped lightly on the door, four sets of eyes looked my way. The only ones I was interested in were the beautiful brown ones, which were the color of silky chocolate.

Reyna was at my side in an instant, her arms wrapped around my shoulders in a tender embrace. "I've missed you. When did you get back?"

"We just got here," I looked over at the mess of papers sprawled across the comforter. "Looks like you girls have been busy."

Reyna turned her head toward the girls. "We are planning my birthday party." Switching her gaze to me, she lifted to her toes before placing a kiss on my lips. "Thank you."

If it was within my power, I would stop at nothing to make Reyna happy, as long as it didn't jeopardize her safety. Releasing her, I left the room and headed down the stairs for the second time.

The men were still gathered around Calvin's computer as I entered the enclosed area. Patton had joined them, and based on the way he was rubbing his chin, something had him baffled. Eager to see what they were looking at, I picked up my pace until I was standing behind Patton. I leaned in so I could get a peek at the screen. My heart fell to my stomach, unable to comprehend what I was staring at.

Pushing Axe and Marcus out of the way, I had to get a better view of the screen for my own sanity. "Where the fuck did this come from?"

Calvin took in a deep breath and said, "It came from a reliable source. It was taken less than two hours ago."

"There is no way this could be real. I saw her. She was confirmed dead." Anger and hurt consumed me as I took Axe by the shirt. "You saw her. The night of her bachelorette party. Gwen was beaten to death."

Torn, I glanced over to the entrance to find Reyna

standing there. "Davian. Was Gwen your fiancée? Is it true? Is she still alive?"

Reyna's words were coated with so much hurt and hopelessness, and I felt like my entire world had come down. Everything pointed to Salko. He staged Gwen's death and took the woman I loved from me. For five years, I mourned her death. He stole the life we were supposed to spend together.

Releasing the grip I had on Axe's shirt, I turned and faced the screen. Instead of answering Reyna's question, I studied the man who was standing next to Gwen. "No matter what it takes, Salko is a dead man."

About the Author

Some would call me a little naughty but I see myself as a writer of spicy thoughts. Being a romance writer is something I never imagined I would be doing. There is nothing more rewarding than to put your thoughts into words and share them. I began writing in 2013, and have enjoyed every minute of it. When I first began writing, I really wasn't sure what I was going to write. It didn't take me long to realize that romance would be my niche. I believe that every life deserves a little bit of romance, a little spice doesn't hurt either. When I am not writing, I enjoy the company of good friends and relaxing with a delicious glass of red wine.

I hope you found The Perfect Escape enjoyable to read. Please consider taking the time to share your thoughts and leave a review. It would make the difference in helping another reader decide to read The Perfect Escape and all of my books.

To get up–to-date information on when The Perfect Lie, book #3 in the Sinful Pleasures series will be released click on the following link **http://bit.ly/2qIoqAY** and add your information to my mailing list. There is also something extra for you when you join.

Sinful Pleasures
The Perfect Wife
The Perfect Escape
The Perfect Lie (March 2021)

The Last Chance Series
Bought
Slaved
Taken
Broken
Freed

Shattered Innocence Trilogy
Next to Never: Shattered Innocence Trilogy
Next to Always: Shattered Innocence Trilogy, Book Two
Next to Forever: Shattered Innocence Trilogy, Book Three

Jagged Edge Series
Hewitt: Jagged Edge Series #1
Cop: Jagged Edge Series #2
Hawk: Jagged Edge Series #3
Sly: Jagged Edge Series #4
Ash: Jagged Edge Series #5
Gainer: Jagged Edge Series #6
Chavez: Jagged Edge Series #7
Ryan: Jagged Edge Series #8

Unbreakable Series
Beneath Deception
Beneath Submission

Standalone
Love Inside the Silence
Sirius: Hidden Truth
Saving Hanna

Keep up with all the latest releases:

Twitter:

https://www.twitter.com/allong1963

Facebook:

https://www.facebook.com/ALLogbooks

Official Website:

https://www.allongbooks.com

GoodReads:

https://www.goodreads.com/ALLong

BookBub:

https://www.bookbub.com/authors/a-l-long

Made in the USA
Middletown, DE
24 October 2023